BLACK DIASPORA

Tales and Poems from the Sons and Daughters of Africa

KINSMAN AVENUE PUBLISHING, INC.
www.kinsmanquarterly.org

Registered with the U.S. Library of Congress
Library of Congress Control Number: 2024900654

Printed in the United States of America

Black Diaspora: Tales and Poems from the Sons and Daughters of Africa

ISBN: 978-1-962121-00-2 Paperback
ISBN: 978-1-962121-01-9 Hardback
ISBN: 978-1-962121-02-6 eBook format

Cover Design by Anastasia Simone
Book Design by Monique Franz and Summer Greigh

Content Editing by Monique Franz
Line Editing by Dawn Leas
Supporting edits by Sophia Obianamma Gabriel
and Mildred J Mills

Contributing authors in alphabetical order:
Bello Abdullahi, Margaret Ajakaiye, Elizabeth Best, Tiara Imani Blain, Carmen Brady-Bronston, Nikẹ Campbell, Odette Cortés, Charmaine Denison-George, Monique Franz, Sophia Obianamma Gabriel, Yakhare Gueye, Akin Jeje, Veripuami Nandee Kangumine, Kay Lopez, Hadija Mude, Nicole Negrón, Blessing Odunyemi, Jody T. Pratt, Quiana, Jana Ross, Abdulrazaq Salihu, Jon Jon Stefan, and Jonathan Chibuike Ukah

BLACK DIASPORA

Tales and Poems from the Sons and Daughters of Africa

Edited by Monique Franz
Co-Editor: Dawn Leas
Cover Design: Anastasia Simone

Dedicated to our African brothers and sisters
dispersed throughout the world.

Editor's Note

I experienced Africa for the first time in April 2011. As a Black American, I lived so far from my African roots that the Motherland seemed almost mythical until I set foot on its soil.

We arrived in Addis Ababa, the capital of Ethiopia—the only African nation that escaped colonization. Everyone looked like family. The faces on all the billboards, magazines, newspapers, and TV screens looked like mine.

The next day, I attended a church service held in Amharic. I sat immersed in the language's music, its beautiful tones, the subtle click that emerged in sentences. I felt desperate to understand it—unlike I ever felt in a language foreign to me. When the congregation broke into a song, I wept and fell to my knees. As the people sang in acappella, it was as though intermingled in the harmonies, I heard my ancestors from generations upon generations call out to me and say, *you are home*. For the first time in my life, I felt like I belonged. And for the first time, I truly understood the brutality of my displacement as a Black American.

The slave trade and colonization stole so much of our story, and this anthology recovers some of the booty, so to speak. The *Black Diaspora* gives us Afro descendants the opportunity to use our voices without a White overseer or master to dictate what we can or cannot say. In many ways, we are still learning how to use our voices, and platforms like Kinsman Quarterly offer Afro descendants a safe space to do so.

This collection shares our fantasies, our horrors, our anger, our love, our desperation, our audacity, our clarity, our confusion, and it is created for us to treasure. We are again using our voices and telling our stories so that Black people dispersed around the world can open the pages and feel a sense of home. —*Monique Franz*

JOURNEY

PAIN

FEAR

LOVE

TRANSCENDENCE

JOURNEY

Section 1

BLACK SNOW

Blessing Odunyemi

The children marveled
as adults clapped
The Black Snow had arrived

Stark contrast to the red clay
that was a little too social
clinging to feet, lungs, faces
The Black Snow had arrived

Hot and sticky smelling
acclimating to the humidity
in which it took residence

It felt strange and sickly
in their chests
but nobody dare interrupt the
celebrations all around because
The Black Snow had arrived

Children stepped foot in its warm softness
like puppies,
apprehensive of their paw prints
They wished to lie down
make snow angels
their parents screamed
"Ma bọ! Ma bọ!"
          The Black Snow had arrived

The thick air intoxicated
leading to music and dance
praise hands upturned because
          The Black Snow had arrived

Paving a new, fresh path of promise
to a future unchanged
and blemished.

SILENT PASSENGER

Nike̩ Campbell

I don't feel the warmth of home. Not even with "Welcome to Nigeria" blaring as I descend the escalator at Murtala Muhammed International Airport. The air conditioning hits me as I walk through the sliding doors to Customs and Immigration. I sail through a line of uniformed officers. Not one demand for a bribe. *That's different.*

Over at the carousel, I place my luggage in a cart with no fuss. Twenty years ago, crowds surged in like avalanches. Heckling travelers demanded to exchange money. Peddlers pimped out the use of their mobile phones for a fee. Not now.

Outside, police pace back and forth. One turns to me.

"You better get home now. Curfew begins at 10 this evening."

Just then, the phone buzzes in my jeans pocket. My hand trembles as I reach for it. Uncle is on the other end.

"Small Madam, welcome home! Give me a few minutes to park. I will come and get you at arrivals."

His voice is just as I recall, deep and gruff.

"No, Uncle. I'll find my way."

"But you're not familiar with the new renovation. The airport has changed."

"It's not a bother," I say.

"Okay. I'll be there in a sec."

Right before my short walk to the garage, I text Stella, my bestie from secondary school. We tell each other everything. I let her know I've arrived safely.

Suddenly, the blue Mercedes slithers up in the parking garage. Uncle's face emerges, wrinkled and shrunken. He wears bushy, grey brows and gaps in his teeth. What's left of his hair is close shaven, but he looks almost the same. He has aged, but only evident in the sagging skin under his chin and the sloping shoulders of his French suit. He jumps out of the car, like a man half his age.

"Princess Ally—a.k.a. Small Madam! Is this you?" Uncle grabs the cart and empties my luggage into the trunk of the car.

I take a deep breath and open the door to the front passenger seat.

"Sit in the back," he says.

"I can sit in front, you know," I say, forcing a smile. "I am no longer a child."

I duck into the passenger's seat. My foot hits an object wrapped in a plastic bag.

"You see? Why didn't you listen to me? Go and sit in the back, young lady."

Embarrassed, I obey. Once I settle in, Uncle adjusts the rear-view mirror. For a few seconds, his glassy eyes lock with mine. I look away.

The headlights of an approaching car fix on us for what seems like an eternity. Uncle freezes. The car then disappears around the corner and up to the next garage level. Only then does Uncle drop his hand and relax his shoulders.

A familiar voice from the radio fills the car. "And in the news tonight, the police are still in search of the elusive—"

Uncle switches the station. Soft jazz fills the car instead. I take deep, slow breaths and exhale, but my quivering hands betray me. I steady them between my thighs, focusing instead on the overhead cement pillars. The walls close in.

I press the automatic window and free my arm as the car speeds from the garage and onto the traffic-free highway.

Uncle steals another look at me through the mirror. He chuckles.

"I can't believe you still do that."

Twenty years ago, as a teenager, I stuck my hand out the car window and waved at strangers. Uncle would pick me up from school and drive me around town. He was our family driver and fancied himself as a father figure. I guess, in some ways, he tried to be.

The house welcomes me back like an old friend. Save for the lingering smell of paint, nothing has changed. Uncle's guest house sits at the edge of the property. I glance at it before turning towards the back door leading into the kitchen.

"Mama is asleep," says the house help. Mercy is from Mom's hometown, *Ikot Ekpene.* She looks all of 15 years old, her hair threaded into Bantu balls. Mercy scurries around the kitchen like a tiny squirrel, industrious and calculated. "She try o, but the medicine she tek make 'im sleep."

Mom's bathroom accident is the reason I am back. When Aunty Aggie called a month ago, I recalled the day of the first car accident involving Uncle and Mom. The two survived. But this time, Mom fell and broke her leg, climbing out of the bathtub. Aunty Aggie expressed her annoyance about the incident.

"It is high time your mother stops living alone and doing everything by herself. She needs a house help."

"Aunty, who will take care of the expenses but me, her only child? I can't afford that."

"It's already a done deal," Aunt Aggie said. "Besides, Uncle has already resumed work as her driver and a house help is arranged with an agency."

I could hardly breathe. "Which uncle?" I asked.

"The family driver from your childhood," she scoffed. "The same from before you went to study in America."

"Why him? Couldn't you have found someone else?"

"Are we not talking of the same uncle?" Aunty Aggie asked. "He is like family, and he needs us now. He has fallen on hard times and only needs shelter and food. His second wife passed just like the first. He has no children or other family to support him in his old age."

Aunty Aggie didn't need to say more. I purchased my ticket for home the same day.

Mercy, eager to show off her culinary skills, ushers me into the dining room where the food waits. She made my favorite, pounded yam and Ẹgusi soup. I enter the dark room where a floor lamp stands in the farthest corner.

"Can you switch on a lamp or two?" I ask.

When no light appears, I turn around. Behind Mercy, Uncle lurks in the shadows.

I gasp, tripping over a cord partially hidden under the rug.

Mercy turns to look behind her. "Ha! Uncle! Why you stand there like that?"

"Sorry. I didn't mean to scare you." Uncle steps under the fluorescent light in the hallway. His eyes dance with amusement.

"I-I'm…sorry," I say to them both, heading upstairs. "I think—I am too tired to eat."

The next morning, my mother doesn't recognize me at her bedside. Aunty Aggie warned me this will happen as it did with their mother. Still, I have not braced myself for the blank look in Mom's eyes when I call her. The fall in the bathtub must have compounded her condition.

Mom sits up, the cotton nightgown loose around her gaunt neck. I am taken aback by the cropped snow-white hair. She finally stopped dyeing it into that unnatural soot color. The low cut, the only semblance of our similarity. Mom is tall and slim, while I am vertically challenged. Where she is outspoken, I am reserved.

I grab her hand on top of the blanket, and the veil lifts from her eyes. She hugs me.

"Have you eaten?"

"Not yet. I wanted to see you first."

Mom's eyes travel to my hair. "When did you cut your hair?" she gasps. "If not for your earrings—thank goodness—you could be mistaken for a man!"

"I know, it's very short," I say. "Mom, why did you let Uncle back here after so long?"

Mom stares at me and bursts out laughing. I don't laugh at all.

My phone rings in my pocket. It is Stella.

"Hey girl. I'm sending an Uber to bring you to meet me at the first location, but for the other places, it will only be you and Rapha." She hesitates for a moment, "One more thing..."

The phone shakes in my hand.

"…there has been another disappearance."

Stella and I meet under the bridge where the makeshift bus stop no longer exists. It is now a garden with an array of flowerbeds, popping with colors.

"Wow!" I comment.

"Beautiful, right?"

It was. The new governor announced during his campaign that he would embark on a beautification and tourism revitalization of the State. Since his appointment, illegal bus stops and garbage hills have been demolished and transformed into gardens and parks.

Rapha waits a few feet away. He looks nothing like he does on Channel TV News. Dressed in a crisp, close-fitted shirt and tailored pants, he would be more suited for the runway.

He and Stella greet one another with a hug.

"And here is my best friend, Alero. Alero, this is Rapha, the district police officer."

Rapha shakes my hand. His hands feel soft.

"The published author of the psychological thriller," he smiles. "It is a pleasure to finally meet you. We appreciate you being here."

"Thank you." I slip my hand from his as my palm moistens with sweat.

"You must have heard of the other missing woman from the mainland. She was in her early 20s, just like the others. She was on her way back from evening mass."

Rapha pulls out his phone. "Can you take a look at the picture?"

A face appears on the screen. Jet-black, curly hair pulled back into a bun, and those unforgettable light brown eyes.

"Is this the first woman you remember?" he asks.

"How can I forget?"

"Do you remember what year you saw her?"

"1988. It was my birthday."

"Scroll through the rest of the pictures. Let me know if you recognize the others. There are 11 more."

For 20 years, I saw those faces and relived the places in my dreams. Each area has changed, except the last, whose street remains untarred with potholes.

Rapha drives his SUV there at a snail's speed. I assume he owns it by the way he mutters each time the bottom scrapes the ground.

The streets still feel communal. Women sit under stalls, selling wares of foodstuffs and plastic trinkets. Children run around, shouting and playing. The men tamper under the hoods of cars balanced on cement bricks while others hang around, shooting the breeze. Not unlike that day twenty years before when Uncle picked me up from school.

I remember that the place was far from home, the farthest Uncle and I had ever travelled.

"Why did we come this way?" I asked him.

Uncle ignored me, peering through the window.

Outside, a woman called to us, persuading us to stop to buy smoked fish, corn, Indomie noodles, and eggs. I stuck my head out of the window, waving at a toddler in pink leggings. The child ran alongside the car as it crawled. The woman's alarmed voice pierced my ears. She ran to scoop up the child and rained abuses on us.

Uncle stopped the car and got out. The woman lowered her head and glared.

"I apologize. Can I do anything? Are you okay?" he asked.

"Just go," she said dismissively.

"Let me drive you," he offered.

"Not necessary," said the woman. She pointed to the moss-covered bungalow a few feet away. It was barely visible as the day transitioned into night.

Uncle pushed a few *naira* notes to her.

"For you and the little one," he said. "What is your name?"

The woman grabbed the notes and pursed her lips.

"You can call me Uncle. What's yours?"

The woman's name was Arinola. I remember her kohl-lined eyes and the blue silk scarf that covered her head. It was long, even after she tied it at the nape. The tail fell to her back, and each time she cocked her head to listen closely to Uncle, the tail made a swishing sound.

Rapha drives me back to the house in the evening, and Uncle stands in front of the gate. He squints at Rapha who comes to open my car door.

Rapha glances towards Uncle and whispers to me, "I'll be waiting."

I nod nonchalantly, as if my head was not whirling from the different locations we had been today. After Rapha drives away, Uncle's eyes dig into my back with suspicion. He follows me into the house.

Aunty Aggie is visiting with mom in the living room. The two sit on the sofa, talking quietly. I sit in the armchair opposite them. As I greet Mom and her sister, Uncle shuffles between the room and hallway. A few minutes later, he appears with two foot stools.

"Ah, Uncle-uncle," Aunty says. "Thanks for putting new legs on these for my sister."

Uncle places one under mom's bandaged foot and the other next to Aunty Aggie's sandaled feet.

"That's what family does," he winks. "We take care of one another."

His eyes rest on me as he pulls out a chair at the dining table and sits down. We all remain quiet, watching the silent TV and its closed captions.

Mom turns to me. "How was your day?"

"Good," I say.

It is easy to lie. Mom remembers Stella. The tale about lunch and shopping is not far-fetched. I dig into the shopping bag Stella gave me.

"I bought these for you, Aunty."

Aunty pulls four separate designs of *adirẹ*, each six yards in length.

"Look at the fine artwork!" Aunty gushes as she turns to Mom. "Look what your daughter got me, o!"

A face appears on the TV screen. A journalist speaks to a reverend father outside of a church. The man's eyes are blood red. I reach for the remote-control on the center table and increase the volume. His voice fills the living room. He begs for information about his missing parishioner.

"She is a devout member of our church," the father says. "She just completed eight years as a fashion design apprentice. Her graduation is in two days."

Mom shakes her head at the television. “What is going on in our world today?”

Aunty Aggie looks up from her designs. “Sister, I don’t know! What do you say to that, Uncle?”

Uncle drums his fingers on the table, then answers with his eyes fixed on me. “The world has always been this way.”

The sisters look at him as if he holds all the answers. Uncle likes to think he does.

Summoning every ounce of strength left, I spring to my feet. “I am going upstairs,” I tell the women, “Uncle…”

Uncle stops tapping.

“Will you please drive me tomorrow morning?” I ask, clearing my throat. “I have an important errand I can only entrust to you.”

Uncle’s lips part, braced to speak, but then they close again. He nods instead, a strange fire smoldering in his eyes.

At seven the next morning, Uncle waits by the car. I arrive later showered and dressed. He grins and opens the back door for me to sit behind him. When he gets in the car, he again peeks at me in the rear-view mirror.

“Ready?” he asks, grabbing the gear. I soon hear rustling paper. I look down at the center console. My novel, *Silent Passenger*, is opened to a page, having a patch of yellow-black cloth draping through it like a bookmark.

Uncle turns around. “I’ve been reading your novel. Actually, I should say, re-reading it for the fifth time.”

I press my phone between my thighs as he drives out of the compound. Mercy waves goodbye from the front door.

“That’s my first.” I smile nervously.

“I know,” Uncle nods once, then honks at the security guard as we near the estate gate.

“And it’s inspired by true events?”

I bite my upper lip to stem the panic flaring up like flames in my chest.

"Yes. Aren't you going to ask where I want to go?"

Uncle looks ahead.

"Tell me about Orela, the main character," he says. "Funny how that's your name reversed. Why did she stay away for so long? Wasn't she afraid the man would hurt her family?"

I swallow the fear and assert my voice. "She knows he actually loves her family too much."

The car accelerates on the highway. I can't tell where we are in the rush hour traffic. Uncle's eyes and mine clash in the mirror. His gaze narrows, as though he found his next prey.

He slows the car down, and we exit the highway. The tick-tick sound of the signal light in the car comes to an abrupt stop. We are now on a side street that is vaguely familiar. I can't disguise my shallow breaths any more than I can unsee the place before me.

I grab the back of his headrest, leaning forward. "No."

Uncle sneers.

The car has stopped in front of a moss-covered bungalow. The compound is empty. I whisper, *Thank God* under my breath, only to swear in the next.

A woman emerges from the familiar house with a baby tied to her back and a broom in hand. She bends and sweeps. He watches her through the slits of his eyes. The swish of the broom reminds me of the sound of Arinola's long scarf, right before she succumbed to Uncle's plea. She left her child with her neighbor that day 20 years ago. Then, she entered Uncle's car.

Uncle turns to me as I marvel at the woman. "I've been following your career. I waited for part two of your series. But you disappointed me by starting a whole different one, a fictitious one at that."

"I needed a break from reality," I told him, narrowing my gaze.

"You needed your muse. Now you can finish it," his grin grows more mischievous. "Answer the questions your readers have been asking for years about Orela."

"What questions?"

"Did she come back to avenge the deaths of the victims? Did she turn the killer in? What became of her?"

My ragged breath blows against his neck as I lunge towards him.

"We are in broad daylight. You, of all people, know better."

"Relax," he says.

I become that 16-year-old girl again. I see the woman, with the child now in her lap. She also sees me in the back seat.

It is the same woman Rapha and I visited yesterday. The woman with the kohl-lined eyes and turban-wrapped head. Yesterday, Rapha asked if she knew Arinola, the missing woman from 20 years ago. The woman stood to her feet, waking the sleeping child in her arms. She demanded to know who we were. Rapha pulled out his badge, introducing himself and his investigation of the deaths of 12 women between 1988 and 1993.

"We think it's linked to the new killings that started a month ago," Rapha told her.

The woman hugged her baby close to her chest, and in between sobs, asked if we had found her mother's body.

As Uncle and I drive away from Arinola's daughter, she and I lock eyes. I place a finger over my lips, hoping Uncle does not see the exchange. I lower myself in the backseat, plunge in earphones, and shield my eyes with sunglasses to avoid the rear-view mirror.

Uncle and I don't speak on the long ride home. All the while, the memories surface. Uncle was never the typical driver. He was a university graduate with good diction. He dressed in French suits and polished leather shoes. The women in our neighborhood swooned over him. He was like the one-eyed man in the land of the blind.

It started with Ruka, the lady with the jet-black hair pulled into a bun and light brown eyes. She waited at the make-shift bus stop under the bridge. I remember she was so small and looked like she needed saving. As the other commuters rushed Uncle's car, begging for a ride in his *kabu-kabu*, Ruka eagerly pressed against the window on my side.

I pleaded for Uncle to pick her up. There was a strange light in his eyes when he let her in. She was shy when he asked her name, as they usually were. She tilted her head towards him when speaking, as would the others after her, and like them all, she paid me no attention.

Uncle interrupts my thoughts. "We're home."

I pull off my earphones. His icy eyes return to the rear-view mirror. I look ahead and realize we are at the house gate. Mercy opens it wearing a familiar yellow wrapper with black swirls. *That pattern?* I look down at the center console. *The fabric!*

I grab the back of his headrest, lunging forward again.

"No. No, not her too."

Uncle plasters a smile on his face but says nothing.

"I saw you, Uncle," I whisper, as though it will keep the truth confined. "I saw you put Arinola in the trunk of the car. Her scarf. It was trailing the ground. I recognized it."

Uncle reverses the car, despite Mercy's shouts to stop. He swerves around and drives out the main gate, out to the highway. I fall back in the seat, my phone pressed between my thighs.

"I know. I saw you," Uncle suddenly blurts. "I saw your reflection in the car window just before you stole away."

"I ran away."

The car approaches an exit. Uncle veers off the highway.

"We were a family until you decided to leave the nest," he says.

"What family, Uncle? You're not even my blood. Mom insisted I call you that out of respect for your age, but...."

He eyes me through the mirror.

"Your mother, you, and I are family. Did I not take care of you like a father after your father's passing?"

"Did you kill the others, too?"

Uncle swerves off the road, then uphill towards the garbage dumpsite. There's a signboard with large markings as a beautification site with a construction start date. Blinded by the sunset and my sunglasses, I am unable to decipher the small letters.

Uncle brings the car to a stop. He turns around with one hand still on the wheel. "The women wanted more from me. They wanted me to leave my family and be with them. I could not have that."

"I was leaving for university anyway, so what did it matter?"

Uncle shrugs. "Everything matters."

"The accident." I whisper, stunned. "The car accident before my travels? You caused that, so I would stay?"

Uncle taps the steering wheel, looking smug.

"But you and Mom came out without a scratch, but I still left."

"You're back now, aren't you?"

My chest tightens as it dawns on me. "Are you referring to mom's new accident? Her broken leg?" I ask. "You were responsible for that? Knowing she wouldn't remember?"

Uncle lowers his eyes. For a split second, I see a vulnerable boy seeking to belong. Then his glare returns in the mirror.

"I always try to be a good husband. I tried to be a good husband to my second wife, and I was—for a while." Uncle looks ahead into the hills of debris.

"You killed her too?"

"Nothing was keeping me there anymore." At this, he turns and smiles. "I've been following your career and waited for years for part two of your series. You need your muse. Now you can finish it."

"Uncle—"

"Now, you can answer the questions your readers have been asking for years about Orela. Did she come back to avenge the deaths of the victims? Did she turn the killer in? What became of her?"

A crazed look emerges from Uncle's eyes as he throws his head back, howling with laughter.

I grab the door handle and pull at the lock. Uncle continues laughing as I tug to break free. A sudden screech of tires quiets him. Squad cars circle us. Uncle's eyes flash with rage.

"You are under arrest!" Rapha's voice blares through the PA system. "Open the door and release the lady now!"

Uncle's face contorts, "You led them to us?"

I pull my phone from between my thighs and show him the screen.

"The police have been listening since we got in the car."

Sirens wail louder.

Uncle smiles as though he is proud of me. Then he opens the door. "This is where it ends, then." He steps out of the car.

I climb over into the driver's seat. "Where are the bodies?" I demand. "Where?"

Uncle turns around with his arms wide.

"Why do you think I brought you here?" he asks. "You are the writer. Finish the story."

Uncle rushes towards the vehicles despite the warnings from the bullhorn.

I close my eyes and brace myself.

THE PILGRIM'S REST

Carmen Brady-Bronston

It was the first day of Spring, March 2023, when we road-tripped
down to your childhood home,
Waze declaring which way to go, edging us out through
Dallas morning traffic, pressing us Southeast
toward Palestine…
Snowy white Dogwoods in bloom, sprinkle the 175 as we pass
into denser prairielands where freshly stacked blue bonnets mingle
amongst golden daisies, all
pushing up from red clay—together… and
defiantly lining verdant ranch pastures,
enclosed, as it were, by flimsy wooden hedging and yet
still rife with promise
and the certainty of Spring…
All this color reminding us,
even as we roll onward—two generations setting
side-by-side—past hectic tides of
Winter and the recollections of yesteryear,

where the times necessitated you turn corners, ducking
in, out, down, and under in the face of a chillier
Hegemony…
these prairies reminding us, too, of those in our lineage
who have gone before,
Felicitia, Lillie Ann, Zenobia and Didi…Ezekiel, Samuel, Jake, John,
and Charlie…
paving paths up, out, and over,
weaving us a future and a hope with the costly currency of
timeworn Forgiveness, even through thorns and thickets,
the back of the bus and pickets,
reiterating again where we've been, of who we were,
and of how far we've come to land and stand freely here
in this tapestry of
a new Day…
Seeds of freedom planted decades prior,
having sprouted, ripened, and dried up
drive us in to remembering a season not long gone, but thankfully, long
Past…
East Texas:
We are written in the fabric of your history even if our weft of the
story has only
traveled by word of mouth from the lips of our ancestors down into
the ears and hearts of our children,
for Mama—there would be no me without you,
and no you without them,
so tell me of your history once again,
lest I forget…

It was the day before Independence Day, July 1948, when you and
your twin brother introduced yourselves
to the world from that country Texas town in Anderson County

—that town known as home to generations of our family,
although yours would be the
Last…
804 Campbell Street,
Palestine, Texas 75801:
Your childhood homeplace, built of brick in the early 50's,
still standing—one story,
three bedrooms, one bath…a kitchen, a great room and
an even greater backyard—even though today,
the grand Paper Shell Pecan tree you plucked from in your
backyard no longer stands,
It, along with the wild blackberry bushes,
cheeky chiggers, and summer grass that line your
memories, will now line mine because you
speak of it…
These once segregated roads you and your three siblings roamed
seemed so broad when you were young: Fulton, Dye, Lacey, Texas Avenue,
New Town, Old Town, your
Daddy's old corner store, and the front steps of Pilgrim
Rest…
Our ancestral line shed sweat here while they lost and kept
progeny there,
Yet they kept moving until they slept,
so that you could find your Pilgrim
Rest…
For me it will ever be more than just a chapel on the edge of Fulton Street…
where you, a six-year-old girl setting on concrete steps,
first laid eyes on my Daddy—a boy six years your senior
who hadn't quite noticed you
(yet).
I am here because you were there…
And so Today, we are travelers setting side-by-side, purveying history

once again,
solidifying facts and relics from one era to the next as we
—the walking, breathing, talking historical markers traverse time, space,
and generations to voice the stories in color that the land
"may" have shut up in black and white…those oralities
that harvesters of history
"may" have forgotten to reap and preserve;
Today, we take pictures on Smartphones and
cross to the "other" side of the
Railroad tracks with no fear,
and with no trepidation…
but rather with our hearts fully set on Pilgrimage
and the Just Promise
of our Pilgrim's Rest.

LIVING WATER

Hadija Mude

The Land Cruiser turned a sharp bend and the family's homestead opened before her. Samira paid the driver and stepped out of the car into the cloud of dust. Her canvas bag in one hand, she removed her sunglasses, hooking them into the neckline of her *buibui*. Standing there, a brilliant smile registered all she'd missed. She walked eagerly through the steel gates nestled between wild, thorny bougainvillea vines, the familiar pink and purple blooms, a resplendent welcome.

The family farmhouse stood at the entrance. Across from it—the well—the homestead's main water source. Samira nearly drowned in it as a child. She jumped carelessly on top of its corrugated iron sheet covers and would've fallen inside were it not for the quick reaction of her mother. It had been a year since she was last home. She stood still and took it all in. The goat pen and familiar stench of dung that clung to the air. She was back home in Isiolo, thousands of miles away from her faculty residence at the University of California's Medical School.

Walking up to the bungalow's door, Samira spotted a figure in the distance. She dropped her bag and quickened her steps in that direction. Then, she stood behind her mother who busily tended the land without noticing her daughter's presence. The old woman wore a brown cotton dress and a matching headscarf. She was barefoot and hunched over, hoeing shallow holes in the ground. She placed a maize seed inside each cavity and covered it with a light layer of soil. Quietly and methodically, she worked in neat rows, the bangles on her wrists playing a dissonant tune.

Samira stood back and admired her mother's industry, fascinated by the old woman's vigor. Her neck craned forward angling for a better view, she was oddly drawn to the backs of her mother's knees. Their dark veins visible underneath the thin, sallow skin. Samira examined the skinny, sturdy legs all the way down to the heels. Cracked and calloused, they looked like the roots of two planted trees. The old woman stood up to stretch and finally noticed her daughter standing behind her. She squinted and held a hand to her forehead.

"Sami?"

"Maamayo!" Samira called out, drawing closer without disturbing her mother's work.

"*Alhamdulillah*!" The old woman beamed. She took her daughter's face in her hands. "*Dhassa tiyya*! We have to celebrate!" she added, pointing to the goat pen.

Samira saw the age in her mother's face. The filmy eyes, the downturned contours of her cheeks, the lines on her forehead.

"*Iyyo iyyo ayyo*! No need! Who will do all that? Samira said. "I'm ok."

Samira was starving but would not trouble her mother with the slaughter and preparation of a goat. Besides, only two of the five in the herd remained, both females kept for their milk, which must have slipped her mother's mind.

"Make for me your rice and beans!" Samira said, picking up her mother's tools and placing them inside a nearby shed. The old woman smiled and took her daughter's hand in hers. They headed for the old faithful farmhouse; the sky stained dusky red behind them.

Samira put her bag away and sank into the living room's sofa as her mother disappeared into the kitchen. When she looked up, her mother was placing a metallic tumbler filled with water on the table before her.

Samira's face grew concerned. "Ma, where is this water from?"

"You must be thirsty! Drink! The bottled water—finished!" the old woman said, shrugging in annoyance.

Samira picked up the tumbler and swished the water out the door. Her mother twisted her mouth.

"I'm sorry, Ma, but that will make you sick! I have clean water." Drying her wet hands nervously on her *buibui*, Samira went into the bedroom and returned with two bottles.

"Maamayo, drink this. It's better." she held a bottle out to her mother who didn't budge.

A week before, Samira's brother Adhan sent her the last of his ominous WhatsApp voice messages.

"Sis, I'm seeing it in the animals. They really want us out. We're at my in-laws in Meru. Mom refused to come with us. She won't listen to anybody. Only to you if you come here yourself."

Going to Isiolo. Family emergency was the extent of Samira's notice to her dean back in California. Much like her professorship, being the eldest girl in an African family was a lifetime appointment, complete with its own set of responsibilities. Her department colleagues, all supportive of her, kindly filled in each time she had to hurry off to Nairobi. Not wanting to worry her aging mother, Samira held off a visit to their rural Isiolo home until after the ruling was made.

"Your Honor, The Gabra people have lived on this land since the 1800s. The Community Land Act protects their rights to live on it and control its resources—"

"Eminent Domain, Your Honor. The Ministry of Lands and Physical Planning intends to build a public school for this community that badly needs it."

The courtroom erupted in murmurs. The elders sat stoic and dignified, with their elaborate kofias and beards dyed red. Samira sat behind them in the crowded public gallery.

The judge peered above his gold-framed glasses, "The court is yet to receive any documents to corroborate the defendant's claim of building a school."

Godana v. Ministry of Lands and Physical Planning. The litigation had gone up to the Supreme Court of Kenya, and a decision was expected to come down in the next few days. Prior to this, Samira had been traveling to Nairobi every three months to represent her family throughout the four-and-a-half years of court wrangling in the country's capital.

Together with her late father's business partners, she assembled an elite legal team, consisting of three property rights lawyers. Two local experts and an American acquaintance whose role, in addition to legally representing the Godana Family, was to liaison with human rights groups to highlight the illegal evictions of private landowners in Isiolo County.

At home that evening, Samira and her mother ate red beans and rice outside on the veranda. They sat under a starry sky, a full moon illuminating their soirée. Insects looped around them, swirling in tandem with the *oud* incense rising from its burner. The old woman now burned the *oud* every day to keep away tormenting evil spirits. Sitting on three-legged cypress stools, the two women laughed, catching up with each other. How was it teaching rich children in America? How was it living alone in the once lively *boma*? How was she managing without the help of her son, daughter-in-law, and two grandsons? Who was she sending to town to fetch her household supplies and fertilizer? It had only been a week since they deserted her, so she managed just fine with her current stockpile.

Samira washed down her meal with the bottled water, her mother opting for goat's milk instead. She drank copiously from its gourd, barely touching the rice and beans on her plate. Her daughter listened quietly as the old woman wheezed and gasped lamentations through the night. She didn't deserve to be abandoned by her family. They'd enjoyed her land and what it produced but left because the county governor had said so. Her son was "spineless," running away, instead of staying to put up a fight. A fight for his rightful place on his ancestral land.

"*Waqqi worbalesina*! God will punish them!" she spat. "We… used to ha—have… resp… ect… for—"

She struggled to finish her thought. A violent cough seized her in a chokehold. Her breathing rasped and eyes watered. The moisture collected in the wrinkles on the sides of her face. The betrayal seemed to get her so upset, she asked to lie down. She would see Samira in the morning. At least somebody in her family had the self-respect to stand up to the land grabbers. The looters didn't "stand a chance" against her American-educated daughter.

Accustomed to waking up early for medical rotations, Samira rose with the first flush of morning. She decided to go on a walk and put on a light *dera*. When she stepped outside, a biting wind lashed at her face, and she darted back in. She had forgotten how cold Isiolo got at that hour.

She rummaged through her nephew's bedroom drawers for a sweater and warm pants, finding both items two sizes too big. She slipped on the pants under her *dera* and threw on the oversized sweater. She fastened her hijab around her face and as she walked out caught a glimpse of herself in the full-length mirror. She chuckled at her ridiculous attire, then stuffed her phone and hands in the sweater's pockets.

She strolled through the scrubland, the yellow blooms of lantana and scent of eucalyptus lining her path. The neighborhood slowly stirred into life. The aroma of morning wood-fires whirled around her. She waved at a woman guiding a donkey-cart, then at a shopkeeper sweeping the front steps of his kiosk, its shutters still closed. A military jeep rumbled past; its GK plates faint through the cloud of red dust in its trail.

Samira walked until she found herself on the crest of a small hill. Having found the perfect vantage point, she tucked her *dera* behind her knees and sat on the dewy grass. With her eyes closed, she took in clean breaths that came out in dense cloudy exhales. She drew her knees to her chest and looked out. Wisps of smoke and rusty-red roofs dotted the vista, along with neat square plots of vegetation. Her eyes swept the landscape in wonder. How lush was her hometown. In the distance stood the silver dome and twin minarets of the local mosque. Further still, the hazy facade of Mary Immaculate, the old Catholic Church. Both buildings, relics of the community.

Isiolo, her home. A crossroads of the nomadic north and agrarian south. Bantus, Nilotes and Cushites; all people groups of Kenya found common ground here. A gateway to the country's northern frontier. A cultural and trading hub. What had happened? Why the sudden rise in political tensions and land disputes? While she was aware of the government's insatiable appetite for privately owned land, Isiolo wasn't part of its typically coveted highlands region.

Bereft, Samira closed her eyes. A mix of anger and sadness coursed through her. She lost touch with the events and developments happening back home. Mutuma, an old college boyfriend, was her only other contact outside of the family. He and she rarely spoke about the area's politics, too banal and unworthy of the international calling rates. They kept it light during those long-distance phone calls. Mutuma would sarcastically ask her when she'd get married. She'd ask him about his wife and children. The two enjoyed each other's banter, trying to forget that theirs was a missed opportunity and platonic "penpalship" must suffice. Mutuma gave his quiet and steady support for her court battle against the government, but she struggled to swallow her pride and ask for his help.

The sun peeked through on the horizon, rising to steam the earth beneath her. Samira rolled up the sweater's baggy sleeves and took out her phone. Hesitantly, she scrolled her call log.

"Mutuma! Hey! *Sasa*!"

"Hhh…hello." A disoriented voice replied.

Samira looked at her phone's clock—6:10 a.m. "Damn! It's early… sorry, I'll call you back—"

"Sam! No no… I'm up! Hi! *Sema*! *Ulicome* when?"

"*Jana*. Just taking care of some things…you know the lawsuit," she replied.

"I saw it on the news. *Poleni sana*. You know we're with you if you need anything."

"Thanks. I'm honestly so scared for mom. She's so attached," Samira said, pinching the wet grass by her feet. "The animals are dying. I just have a bad feeling."

"It'll be ok. You have a whole community behind you. They can't shake us!" he vowed. "*Tutawashow*!"

Samira smiled, emboldened for the real reason of her call.

"I need a favor, Muts. About Mom—she doesn't sound good. Do you mind stopping by to check on her? Bring everything you can?"

"Of course! No problem, I can do that. Meanwhile, relax. *Sawa*? *Usistress*."

A woman's raspy voice called his name in the background. Samira cringed.

"I'll be there later today, *poa*?"

"*Poa*. Thanks!" she quickly replied and hung up.

Samira bit her bottom lip, desperate and a little embarrassed, calling him so early. But Mutuma was well connected, and she needed all the help she could get.

She stood up to take in one last panoramic view, when the muezzin's melodic call to prayer suddenly engulfed the atmosphere. The soulful summons a fitting soundtrack to the breathtaking scenery. She lingered for a few moments, now in high spirits, but feeling too warm underneath the layers of clothing. She removed her sweater, tying it around her waist, then began a slow walk home.

Someone must have slipped the note through the barbed wire fence. Or maybe they walked right in with it. The gate was closed but never locked. It lay conspicuous; bright white and encased in a plastic sleeve, a rock placed to secure it. With twitching hands, Samira picked it up and scanned it, mumbling the words under her breath as she read.

"Judgment in the case of Godana v. Ministry of Lands… the Supreme Court of Kenya… unanimously upholds… in compliance with… section 52 of the Mining Act No. 12 of 2016… the defendant's right to exploration and extraction of mineral deposits… in and around the above mentioned location… Plaintiff is advised to take action now to avoid destruction of property… will be compensated in due course…

Failure to comply… face grievous consequences… including but not limited to—"

Samira fretfully looked around, as though the sender hid somewhere watching her. Notice in hand, she broke into a run, looking for her mother through the compound. Her mother sat by the fire of the three-stoned hearth, outside behind the kitchen. She prepared the morning's tea in the smoky method she preferred, never using the gas stove Samira bought her a few years ago.

Her mother looked up at the sound of the urgent footfall. Breathless, Samira stopped in front of the old woman and mutely held the notice to her face. Not that her mother could read it, much less understand its legal jargon.

"Samira? *Maaan tann*? You don't say good morning to your mother?" The old woman's brows furrowed in concern.

"Maamayo! It's over! It's over!" Samira howled, plopping herself beside her mother at the hearth. Her head hung and her face ashen before its ashes. "*Yaaaa Rabbi*! *Yaaa Rabbi kiyyaaa*! They won!" she wailed, sobbing loudly. Her shoulders heaved with the weight of the decision. The years spent fighting, only for the result to be handed down so casually and callously. Her mother held her daughter close, saying nothing. Samira cried and cried until the old woman's *garbisar* drenched with her grief.

Finally, Samira wiped her tears with her *dera* and turned to meet her mother's eyes. "Ma, do you know what this means?"

The old woman shook her head and went back to stirring ginger and cloves into the bubbling pot of tea, its fragrant steam rising.

Her daughter sought her eyes in the haze of the smoky room, "Maamayo! This is serious! They will destroy everything if we don't leave! It says so right here!" She nearly punctured the piece of paper with her index finger. Her mother was unmoved.

Samira looked down at the notice in her hands, running a thumb over the court's seal stamped at the bottom of the page. Its bumpy ridges felt like the goosebumps over her body. She imagined the five justices of the Supreme Court in their wigs and blood-stained robes. Had any of them come from a place they loved and respected?

"They have poisoned the water. The well. It's not safe. Nothing is safe. You saw how the animals died. They want us out! *Tafadhal* Maamayo! For our safety! Let's just go!" her voice soared. Her mother remained unaffected.

The old woman sat up and fastened her *garbisar* around her face. "Samira. This is my home," she said calmly, thumping her chest.

Samira stood up and dusted the dirt and ash off her clothes. "I'm so sorry," she whispered hoarsely before retreating into the bedroom to rest her pounding head.

She awoke to a knock on the door. Jetlag kicked in as soon as she laid down earlier.

Mutuma! She shuffled into the living room to receive him.

"Hi you! *Niaje*!" she perked up at the sight of his round face offset by his square tortoise shell glasses. His presence was still as calming and pleasant as she remembered it.

"Sam!" Mutuma said, reaching for a hug. The two friends embraced. When inside, he sat on the sofa with his medic bag, and Samira sat across in a rocking chair.

It was a relief to see her oldest friend and confidant. The two had once been Eastern Province's top high school students, both from the same district of Isiolo. Having been accepted to the University of Nairobi's School of Medicine, they both bonded over their shared hometown and love for the Sciences. But their paths diverged when a scholarship opened up at UC Berkeley, and Samira went to pursue a PhD in epidemiology. Mutuma, loyal to the soil, took a dream job at Isiolo's District Hospital. At 42, he was now the youngest medical director in the institute's history.

"Muts, they won. Those thieves won!" Samira began, burying her swollen face in her palms.

"It's an injustice!" Mutuma said, reaching across the table to hold her hand. "I'm so sorry. We will go to the East African Court of Appeals!"

"The worst part is Mom *haelewi*! She doesn't understand how far these people will go. What do I do? She won't drink bottled water, *yaani* everything is a fight—" She held back the tears.

"Water is a serious issue. We're seeing so many cases," he added. Samira worried at a loose thread on her *dera*, "You remember my brother Adhan? He left packs of AquaMist, but she won't drink them, as long as the well—"

A sound broke the conversation. Her mother was coughing. The persistent, strained hacks rang through the house. The two looked at one another, a sense of foreboding between them. They shot up from their seats, rushing to the old woman's aid in the kitchen. The mother slumped over the sink, one arm supporting her head, the other holding her chest. Like lashes across her back, the coughs violently whipped her, bringing her to her knees.

"Ma!" Samira leaped to her mother's side, catching her tumble to the cement floor. Samira tried to prop her up, but her mother lay prone, writhing in agony.

"Mmm…mhhh," the mother groaned, her breath labored. Shallow puffs rattled in her chest as the coughs waned to sniffles before they finally stopped. Samira sat on the floor with her mother's face in her hands. She thumbed away the moisture in the corners of the old woman's mouth.

"You're ok, Ma… you're ok," she whispered, cradling her mother's head, her headscarf askew to expose strands of thin, grey hair.

Samira and Mutuma helped the old woman to her feet. Her arms loosely in their grips, they walked her down the narrow hallway into her bedroom.

"*Yoya* Mama," Mutuma greeted tentatively as he sat his ex-girlfriend's mother on the soft mattress, lifting her legs off the ground. She offered a strained smile in reply. Samira held her mother's hand while Mutuma retrieved his medic bag from the living room.

He drew out a stethoscope. "Breathe in and out, Ma. As best as you can."

The old woman's lungs crackled in the room's silence, as he moved the disk over her chest and back. After conducting the auscultation, he rested the device's ear tubes around his neck and reached back into the bag for a sphygmomanometer. He delicately wrapped its cuff around the frail upper arm, then set the stethoscope's disk in place and replaced its ear plugs. He pumped the cuff, and she anxiously shifted on her elbows as it bulged around her arm.

Mutuma reassured her with a smile, which the old woman obliged with the fondness she always had for him. Gently, he released the sphygmomanometer's air and carefully listened to her heart.

Next, Mutuma handed her an open specimen container. "Spit into this," he said.

"Samira, what is all this?!" her mother scoffed, making a sweeping gesture with her hand.

Samira, standing arms crossed in a corner of the room, reassured her mother it had been a while since her routine physical. This was merely a formality.

The old woman spat into the container, a guttural glob, and placed it into Mutuma's gloved hand. He closed it, sealed it in a cellophane pouch, and slid it into a slim compartment of the medic bag. He tossed his gloves into a trashcan and handed a bottle of water to her.

"Here you go, Ma. Clear your throat."

The mother took it, placed it on the night table beside her.

"So? What is wrong with me?" she asked the doctor.

"I'll take your sample to the hospital, Ma. We should have answers in a week's time."

As Mutuma gathered his things, the old woman asked him about his family. She then told him that the government was harassing a poor widow because they suspected that her ground might have gold or some other precious thing she didn't know. Mutuma listened respectfully.

"Everything will work out in the end," he said, before they left her alone to rest.

In the following days, Samira's mother grew weaker. One afternoon, she asked her daughter to accompany her out into the field to survey the new crop. Samira gladly indulged for she loved the land and had a stake in it. She had helped her parents plant their crops from six years old, dropping seeds into the two-inch planting holes, covering them with her small but determined hands.

Her late father, an astute businessman and farmer, grew maize, beans, capsicum, and lucrative passion fruit. He made the four acres profitable enough to see his children through high school and beyond. No mean feat in an area where most people didn't get to go to high school, let alone finish it. Her older brother, Adhan, graduated from the teachers' training college in Machakos. Samira from the University of Nairobi's Epidemiology master's program. The farm had fed, clothed, educated, and sustained them. The piece of earth was their lifeline.

Here it was now, stretched out before them. The two women walked its periphery, admiring the bright green maize sprouts, jutting timidly above the moist fecund soil. Her mother shooed away a grasshopper camouflaged on one of the leaves. Samira giggled at the old woman's protectiveness. The rains had just fallen, and the scent of wet earth filled them with joy and gratitude.

A few paces in front of them, under the shade of a guava tree, her father's final resting place. His epitaph read, *Beloved Abba.* Standing there in the homestead's tranquility, Samira felt a sudden surge of tenderness for her mother. Widowed for a few years now, the old woman did well for herself. She kept the farm running, albeit only now for subsistence. She had every right to be proud and rigid. Samira understood her resistance but was also prepared to acquiesce to the government's avarice and save her mother the shame and cruelty. With a tenured academic career and no dependents, she had enough resources to support her. She had offered to relocate her to the neighboring Meru Town and buy her a new piece of land there. All efforts to persuade her mother, ultimately, in vain.

The two walked halfway along the farm's edges when they stopped and looked out. Green as far as the eye could see. In the rolling distance, barbed wire braced by wooden posts separated their farm from others. Long-time neighbors and friends with whom they'd communed in the use of farm equipment, fertilizer and even labor, like pulling each other's weeds.

A few women finished up the planting for her infirmed mother. The well-worn footpaths between the *bomas*, a testament to camaraderie.

But things changed. Day laborers and farmhands left in droves to find work in the cities. There was the constant push by the government to sell! Sell! Sell! The pressure loomed like a specter, and most people, eventually, sold. If only to escape the threats and heavy military presence in the area.

Happy with their budding crop, the two women sought the shade of a nearby tree and sat at its feet. Silently, they reveled in the gift of mother nature's beauty. With hushed ease between them, they each drifted off into peaceful daydreams.

A murder of crows shrieked in the distance, breaking their reveries. The old woman turned to look at her daughter; her filmy eyes shrouded in terror.

"You think I'll be ok?"

For the first time, Samira sensed her mother's fear. She reached for her hand and squeezed it. "Of course, you'll be ok, Ma."

"That Mutuma still loves you, Samira. I don't know what he was thinking, not asking your hand."

Caught off guard by the cheeky quip, Samira looked at her mother and burst into hearty laughter! "Haaaaahahaha!" The old woman joined in, startling the sparrows on the trees and sending them scurrying up into the cloudless skies.

Doubled over, her mother coughed and wheezed from the laughter. Then, she nudged her daughter, feigning seriousness, "*Ila, wosigafado*? When are you getting married?"

Her daughter smiled in amusement. They both knew the answer was likely never. Samira dedicated her life to public health. Teaching it at Berkeley was her greatest joy, and her mother made it possible. Her mother who defied cultural norms, allowing her daughter to follow her academic dreams. Even when those dreams carried her to distant unfamiliar lands. Samira cherished this time spent together with her. A breeze brushed up against her cheek, and she made a mental note to visit more often.

"You're funny Ma! Let's go inside and eat," she said.

Samira stood, holding out a palm to her mother, who placed her hand in hers. The old woman suddenly lost her grip and fell back on the ground.

"*Uuuwi*!" she jerked and coughed in fits. Hunched over, she braced for more of the attack. The booming coughs, in the homestead's silence, echoed into the distant hills. Her mother held on to her chest and lay face down, curled into a ball. Samira crouched next to her, supporting her upper body on her lap.

"Ma! Breathe! Breathe!" she pleaded. Her mother wheezed and gasped for air as Samira struggled to help her sit up. "*Eeh ayyo tiyaaa*!" she wept.

In the frenzy, Samira yanked off her hijab, fashioning a headrest. The old woman dragged at her tired airways and gagged uncontrollably until something released.

"*Ptho*!" She finally spat to expel the blockage!

A large, clumpy mass. The old woman caught her breath. Samira looked. There, on the patch of bare earth beside them, blood. It seeped into the crimson soil, almost imperceptible.

Samira's phone buzzed in her skirt's pocket. It's Mutuma! She quickly answered.

"Muts!" Samira cried. "Mom is coughing up blood! She's coughing up bloooood!"

"I'm so sorry, Sam—" Mutuma said with hesitation in his voice.

"What…What is it? Is it mom's tests?"

"Yes… Unfortunately—" his voice cracked. "We saw abnormal cells in her sample."

"No! It can't be! It can't be it! Don't say it! No! No!" Samira burst in anguish. Her world spun as the crows circled low.

"Sam, I'm sorry, but it's esophageal," Mutuma said. "It's the water."

PAIN

Section 2

CLAY PEOPLE

Jana Ross

We are clay people who bake under the sun
When the brown glistens
And all I can see is your beautiful darkness
I forgot how brittle and hard we be
We, who began as a soft mould,
As life from the bottom of rivers,
Of water, the force of shape and change,
But now, no longer do you let softness in
For the elements set and stiffened arms,
Fingers, backs, and minds, too
Until the rinds of the heart met rigor mortis,
And skin withered to tough leather,
And touch became alien.
In these moments of hardness
Between us family

Jana Ross

I remember these memories we relive,
When our ancestors had to lose trust
And instead gain caverns, boulder shells, and
Pluck for their hearts immovable stones
Submerged in an endless ocean,
They had to look for sunlight
Five thousand meters beneath the surface
Beneath the surface

Our mothers and fathers hid joy and panic
And instead emerged covered in the sand of the ocean floor
But their mud covering also hid what was only meant for special eyes
A beautiful coral held like bouquets
A calling to the sea I know now is a gift from them to me

I remember, too, the quiet smiles that pass through your eyes
The ones I hear in your laugh
And the watery tears slipping to the corners of your lips,
Letting slide a smile oceans wide
In those gentle moments,
When we hold each other and that is all we need,
I remind you softly to think of those before and next,
Us,
And ask for you to let go of these stone walls
Let dissolve this tough, old clay of armor
To wash gently away your pain,
Hold firmly for we are each other's protectors.

HOLD MY BROKEN BOY TOGETHER

Sophia Obianamma Gabriel

Tobe has a scar that rends his face in half, and Emery knows how it came about. At first, the two told people he was Humpty Dumpty reincarnated. It helped that he was bald as a baby's bum since university. Now, they do not joke about it. Time marinated the pain, and silence is the only acceptable discourse.

Tobe loves a White girl, Jessica, whose expatriate father stares too long at his scar. Emery knows the beginnings of a bad story when she sees one. Although Tobe makes no fuss about why his girlfriend looks at her baby brother with a mother's love, or why her father watches the boy with poorly concealed loathing, Jessica's curiosity, especially regarding the scar, is a condiment for disaster. Tobe does not talk about it. To talk about it opens the wound.

Jessica loves Tobe like Ezra loved Emery, yearning to unravel a mystery. One hidden in his deep eyes that pull you in and let you go as he wishes.

Tobe's ears fold in on themselves, slight enough to prevent his bald head—the perfect bald head—from looking like a caricature. His intelligence and sultry voice blot out his flaws, the slight limp and imperceptible lisp. The scar, however, greets the gaze first. And though most remain polite enough not to ask at the first meeting, the eyes are sentient. Those who meet him can't resist trying to trace his story.

It is a muted one. One of the shunning of brothers.

A lorry smuggling goods from Cameroon orphaned Tobe after his tenth birthday. His family was on a trip to Enugu to visit his mother's brother, who had just received his work visa for a job in Canada.

Tobe survived because the collision tossed him out the open window before the car crashed down onto the rocks. His uncle took him to Canada, and Nigeria became a distant memory.

When Tobe arrived in Canada, a lanky child whose hair started to fall out, Emery took him under her wings and told on the black kids who made fun of him. The White kids knew to stay away and talk behind their palms. But the Black kids, cool as they considered themselves, were raucous.

Emery suffered Tobe's silence until he told her about his family. About his youngest sister, who followed him like a duckling, calling the envy of the middle child to him. About his father's promotion and how they celebrated in the parlour until midnight when their legs ached from dancing and their stomachs distended by jollof rice. Although she had questions herself, Emery did not tolerate ignorant questions thrown at Tobe by his peers.

"Did his father really drive a car?"

"What happened to the elephants they rode?"

"Did he know what soap was in Africa?"

"Was his hair falling off because he didn't wash it?"

"Could Africans really communicate with apes?"

Tobe levelled them all with a look from under his thick lashes before he sauntered away.

"Hey, voodoo guy" became anthemic and stuck until high school, where it took on a different meaning. He was undoubtedly beautiful, able to bring anyone under his spell.

When Tobe asked his uncle why they were treated differently, even when the community was Black, Tobe received a response he did not understand then.

"The thing is—a Black man living in America, Tobechukwu, is not the same as a Black American. There is a large difference."

Tobe did not see the distinction. Emery's skin was as black as his, and Tobe spoke like every other kid on the block.

In Tobe's final year of university, a neighborhood allegation of rape brought the taunts back. There were elementary level questions.

"Do African men rely on rape to get a woman because they are too ugly?"

There were riddles.

"Is your uncle unmarried because he has a certain predilection?"

There were strange calls and painful shoves in restaurants.

These remained long after the court ruled it was not rape; long after the woman publicly apologised; long after, his uncle retired into himself and his home. These remained until Tobe's hair would not sprout again, even in tufts. They continued until Tobe broke a bottle on a boy's head for asking if he helped his uncle hold the lady down.

Tobe refused to be punished by law, choosing instead to accept the wrath of large Black boys with baseball bats.

The slander probably didn't stop, but when Tobe returned to Nigeria, he could no longer hear it.

When Jessica's father gets the nerve to ask about the scar, Tobe freezes, but Emery humours the old man with a wink.

"He plays superhero in his spare time," she said. "Super-secret, so that's all you're getting."

Noting the hardness in Emery's gaze, they choose to talk about other things. Tobe's palm rests atop hers before a grateful squeeze.

When Jessica asks Emery why she followed Tobe to Nigeria when Canada was her home, Emery's words are stuck to her throat. She never needed a reason to follow Tobe to Nigeria. His home was her home. And if she was being honest, he was her home.

Tobe playfully pinches Emery's cheeks, and in that silky baritone voice, he says, "Because she is Dora the Explorer, and I'm her backpack."

Emery can't help but notice Jessica's frozen smile, as though she finally understands the lifelong companionship forged by years of unbridled, untainted friendship.

When Tobe and Emery rise from dinner to leave, Jessica kisses the scar on Tobe's face. It is a crack she cannot shut.

BLAME THE GODS

POETRY COLLECTION

Jonathan Chibuike Ukah

I orchestrated the crimes of my ancestors,
and blamed the future for arriving with hope;
no need to blame me for walking away.
I asked for an evening without rain and storms,
but you sent me streaks of lightning and thunder.
I sent out word through every bird in the sky
to send me longer days and shorter nights;
but in your magnificence, you stacked up my fears
blessing me with shorter days and longer nights.
When I asked for a garden of flowers
you sent me a dark forest of marshmallows.

I walked away from you searching for love—
away from these channels of blood and death—
where seas and oceans spread to meet the sky,

where nights cooed in the womb of the day,
where each possibility was a ramp for the impossible.
Yesterday has no power to cancel or change
the vestiges of light tomorrow put in motion.
I have activated my refuge in benevolence
though I am not a refugee but a free-born—
a returning child to the household of his father
who paid bloody ransom to bring him home.

These twilight days have reshaped you into a mirror
lulling the moon to monitor anywhere I go.
But the moon is my mentor and will not succumb
into spitting out its secrets to witnesses of untruth—
the papacy of falsehood, carnal priesthood,
swimming in carnage or serial sacrifice.
Pained pythons groaning in the wilderness
reminds me of the days I knew no miracles,
when we smelt of fear while rushing to the shrines,
passing through graves of hope overgrown with weeds,
passing through paths where leaves were your eyes.

A Brief History of Nostalgia

Your face tangles inside me
a corpse dangling in a closing grave.
You kiss me with clumpy lips
filled with red-blooded worms,
mouth with the fragrances of acetone.
You touch me with your damp hands
holding sliced daisies and roses,
rough and crumpled like rags in a pond.

Often, I stretch out my rough hands,
to pluck you from the leaf-covered grave
where the black iris grows like arrows,
where you smell like a peony, wafts of jasmine
mixing with my hunger and desire.
Your shadow nestles at my side,
melting crocuses and salvia, lilies and roses.

I wanted a solid eternity with you,
and I would not be frightened by life.
The grave is filled with rotten daisies.
Bodies dissolve in a slimy syrup
while I stand in the wild wind—desolate,
desperate and dire—in a deep-hugging valley.
I remind you of how we frolicked,
giggled, laughed, held trembling hands.
Life was a garden of daffodils, a lawn
of purple hibiscuses and yellow orchids.

I have dying crocuses in my mouth,
and pieces of dead wood in my eyes.

Jonathan Chibuike Ukah

I am the shadow of crackling Iroko trees
lumbering over your clustered grave.
I kissed you with broken bottles—spilling songs,
spitting shards of glass on your tongue.
When you spoke, I didn't know
that you would be my pot of despair,
my river singing of deserts and sand.

So, I came to read Paradise at your side,
sprawled in the garden of purple hibiscus;
your hair was thick like the dark forest Durukwu.
We met where the sun built a shelter,
where your blink was a lingering song.
Now I see your shadow everywhere I go—
your breath blowing into my yawning mouth—
where the grass hums your favourite song,
where you have become a river and an ocean.

This emptiness is my footprint on your grave,
the dry token I drop at your grieving side.
I packed my heart to travel to you
and arrived with a thousand suitcases,
a bottle of deep, blue clouds, yellow sky,
a closed and damp Bible, a haven of shadows,
perhaps to wake you from this deep sleep.
I close my eyes, open my dripping mouth
and inhale fresh-minted dews from your grave.

Suddenly, I wake from my slumber,
and it was all a dream, this bucket wish,
this desire to end kissing the nook of your neck
and dim the frequent glow from your eyes.

Though I walk through the valley of death
I will fear no lurking shadows, no falling knives,
no teasing daggers in the shape of lilies.
I shall not leave our children empty
nor render them orphans in their youth.

I refuse to crumble with you or surrender
this dazzle of light at the end of the chasm,
though my desire is more than I can bear;
and I lie on the cesspool of my sweat, Africa,
a fragment of the deep love we shared.
I shore up these thoughts against the time
when I will become a pillar of death, a skull,
a memorial for our children in stasis,
some shards of our broken glass, a fragrance.

A Brief History of Nostalgia, Part 2

Tell me, you who dwell in my silent thoughts,
if it is wrong to remember things past?
To remember your eyes when falcons sing of the sky,
or the crash of my anointed tongue at the empty air,
when your soft voice falls silent in the evening wind,
my afternoons smirched with broken rhythms?
Is it wrong to remember the scent of your words;
when anger smeared your lips with soft quivering
and a trembling mouth no longer uttered harsh words?
There was sadness in the laughter of the people,
the day the crow splattered us with its faeces,
our jackets steeped in red blood from its eyes,
and the rain dropped down its shattering drone.

I remember the night the sun visited us in disguise
wearing a hood to peep into the darkness;
it was there to admire the fragrance of your presence
and vowed to shine brighter than ever before.
How many flowers? How many roses and crocuses?
I can't count the lilies, orchids, daffodils and tulips.
Those whose nights blasted with your memories
have left them at our door as their Thanksgiving.
Is it wrong to remember the lightness of my spirit
when every part of my room smelt of your breath,
and your eyes, flashing like a lavender field,
turned each night of your life into beams of light?
If I am wrong, then I err to have left at all,
leaving me with these memories that never die.
Do not think of me, Mother, do not remember, please
where no memories catwalk is where peace accrues.

A Changeling

If I were a changeling child
I would have come to you like a stranger.
With fire in my mouth, I would have lured you
to follow me where the axis of the Earth
had turned to the path of its origin, its head
steeped to the ground like an overturned tree.
The moon would have appeared to me in the day,
the stars would have wept for me in the morning.
Perhaps I could have seen the sun smiling at me,
when I danced naked at the market square,
because I have a declaration for you.
The friendly rose would have raised an eyebrow,
as aspen leaves sucked the vapours of tomorrow's rain.

At the gathering of the dragonflies,
I complained about your absence;
raindrops drenched my cheeks,
as I moaned at the sun's decay.
I feel my teeth teetering on the edge
after I have eaten sour grapes,
but I have recovered from the shock
of casting you against the moon.
My hunger and thirst; my thrill and trills,
pay tribute to how much I needed you.
I could not hear the melodies of the nightingale
when the screams of the owl pierced my ears.
I have sought you among the changeling.

I have come to love the blast of the night—
it's my welcome song, the hurdle of my quest,

the valley in whose water I soak my body,
stretch my feet and let my blood run through my lungs.
I was swimming in the haze of the day
wallowing in a maze, a labyrinth of confusion and loss,
a peal of despair wringing my hands to desperation-
though that was before tomorrow, the upsurge of joy,
before I decided to come home in search of you.
Because of you, because you are there, I am home.
Now I can stand the burst of my soul,
exceeding the crazy speed of light,
and my cup of happiness will run over.

EXIT WOUNDS

POETRY COLLECTION

Abdulrazaq Salihu

Who called your name and put your body
in this wrath of a game?

The day the world justified calling a spade
a spade, did they also agree that your body
was not worth the beauty?
I know a lot about wounds and scars.

I know how scars are the only certificates
you get for surviving this war between
yourself and all the dark spots this
cleanser couldn't rid off your skin.

I let what I know call me ignorant,
then I carry the wailing of ghosts in my chest.
I run these hallucinations into my skin

till they're real, till I can hold their
hands and spell their bodies into stardust.

I cleanse my body of our sins and watch the nights
put a "RIP" tag on all the people the universe has
ripped out of our chests and
isn't this the essence of Beauty—
to never last forever?
To be a body of pollination today
and collect your withering inside your
mouth like a butterfly bereft of essence?

Like a corpse, swelling to the rhythm
of sadness—to be the threshold towards
light today and watch tomorrow's darkness
spot your skin?

You call the ghosts and you are your own graveyard.
You carry the scars and your wound;
fresh; cut clean: Your tenderness:
a paper-prayer folded into your sick
mother's front teeth; her aching forehead;
the long dance of slavery between her feet
and the ground: the sad rowing
of all the beautiful boats you've grown
to know, into oblivion: Love; all the time: love.

I let go of the ghosts; the people in my head
my father, like a river voyaging garlands,
I let them flow,
unstoppable in their pursuit for
beauty and tenderness.

Self-Portrait as the Night and Morning Phases of the War

"I know what I've seen of blood & death—what the night forgets to cover in its shadows; what part of paradise a bullet undresses before the body, before stealing light from its eyes."
—Abu Bkr Saddiq

The leaking of smoke started from my body.
Our home later succumbed to the music
of the fire, this is how every tale ends—at the climax
of its beginning. In the quiet of the night, your face

Crepuscular, the stars put a stop to the creaking of birds
Our destiny in the hands of a painter, we're oil paints.
We're dark skinned, yet someone can still match our
existence to the precision in the shooting of a deer

By our long-gone ancestors. The story goes, we're
in the middle of the second world war where the
land opens its aches to delft, the small stones
rub against each other the way strangers in the

Subway do—arm rubs against another arm and
nothing human is felt, just urgency—to continue moving.
Story goes, the nights unfurls its ruin, all its inflorescence
making way for revelations and quiet all at once.

Our breaths are not supposed to touch, our hands
are in their own existence, there's a glitch in time
A folding of a heart into oblivion, into a pause, a coma
A whole different world of endless possibilities.

Dawn begins its own cracking, the first crow to mark
the beginning of day is shot mistakenly by a hunter.
Some say it's a bad omen, others are too busy with movement.

I'm cleaning the stain my mother's stain remover couldn't rectify.
I'm avoiding all the dark spots on my own skin,
trying to not remember the one thing my mother
got in a fistfight against the wind—a soft blow beneath the eye.
Call it a cloudage of storms—where my father was the wind.

My first encounter with the police—fear-black-skin against
a White wild social menace, the officer didn't need to see
my complete credentials to tag me guilty, a criminal lost
in his pursuit for corruption. I got cuffed because I was at the

Wrong place at the wrong time. Recited psalms the best way
I knew how to—by starting with my late father's name.
There's what fear does to a man that I must forget.

Let it not be respect, let it not be humility, because
all the things I've feared have never really left me.
All the wrongs I've done, I , master of my beautiful
sins, I wear them when I have to.

On December 5th of a certain year before I knew
what I never knew of my body, I mistook the scars
for home, the spots on my skin for birthrights.
There's certain news about a lost cyborg in the wind.

Nobody is humane or worried, a cyborg would always
be a cyborg. I watch how the news unplug my mother's
ears from reality. I'm stuck with her today because I sought

a reality TV show, not this seer of bad news; overseer of evil.

I only talk to the wind when men love men. In a strange part
of the world I have started a thread for all the things I'd never forget.
After the war, my name is first on the list. *Ya rabb,* you have
given me the light, and you have darkened the path.

My people are lost in their own mind games. I'm afraid
of starting a journey I know nothing about.
There's a slight cut on my skin. There's a smoke gathering.
I haven't begot a thing of my own—only this gas

of transformation to call my own. I haven't begot a thing
to call my name, and I can't help but burn what only
is a part of me, because all the things I fear
Are only growing deadlier now.

Abdulrazaq Salihu

The City of Ghosts is the City of My People and the Only Place I'm Certain of Being Called an Outcast

All the people I love are the ghosts that hunt at night.
The drive to my people's home, the silence of nights
quiets down as the horror fades away. On the roads
you do not meet the drunk, nor do you mistake
the roads paranormal bending into light—a symbol of
purity. It's a thousand hours of walk, your body is
forced into gun powder (and your insecurities
creak into the back of your ear like a broken omen—
clay plates falling on Christmas Eve). Smoke
becomes fire. Your body is an explosion of wrath
on all the wrong planets. Your mother's body is
the first place to hold unto the warmth on the atlas.
You have never known the music of loss so well.
You open your creased palm to cup your withering.
You have never known the value of your beauty
so you let the air-gas-fist slide. You slit the bottom
throat. Let the blood run into its suffering. Let the
body of lifelessness sleep—in heavenly peace, like
silent nights, like holy nights, like all is calm.
You do not know and would not know
all backs that bow must also dance to the ache of
frustrations and anger and fear and despair and
the air in the wind grinds your nostril into an
ammonium confirmed compound of loss.
You do not choke and you do not falter.

A street with ghosts must only gather
a confederation of darkness, your skin
kind is the first to assemble. Ghosts are Whites.
So even in this holy ground, you're discriminated.
You leave the one place that calls you son. Two
roads diverge in a yellow wood. You take none.
You take all. You cling to the illusion of righteousness.
You put your hand again, today, against all the odds.
Yet, you cannot count yourself among your people
and you cannot clasp and not shake in silence.
So all the night's music lay quietly before the soft
lip of the broken town of ghosts and my kinsmen.

Self-Portrait with a Bloodbath

The first to be cut is the one
with the thinnest skin or the
one with the slowest dodge skill.
I was cut   like saw against the skin of wood
I saw my body on the map   slipping into a river
danced the whole night with my crew, burying
the remains of lost and forgotten night people
while the boys compared the water that drowned
and the one that quenched thirst—told them one
was needed, while the other was needy.
I'm dying as the first man to be cut, skin
wide open   like my country's vulnerability.
Skin wide open   like my mouth, aching for
despair. The wound is fresh and the war continues.
I bit my teeth and struggled to cut one man
before I find my peace with the sands.
The earth says, "if a king falls, ten men must fall."
There's a slight crack in the calabash.
There's a slight chance that my cheek may bloom.
My memories would not separate from lost
so the calabash forgets its duty to hold
and pours its anger on us. The flooding
began. I'm the softness of my limb.
I'm angles with stop-lines. Spot
the fault lines, a click between their heads
and blood is the next big thing. Outside the edge
of the town, at the slow waving music of the river
Mamii heads to swim and the people of anger
were there.   Mamii did not swim. Mamii
drowned. I was the first to tell. I was the first

to be told. When there's a cut, the first to feel
the pain is the one cut.   I have been learning
to cut my whole life.   Give me this bloodbath—

Amin.

Abdulrazaq Salihu

Untitled Gen Z Poem about all the Beautiful Places Growing into Cracks

On the day I pushed the sun by its forelimbs away from my
skin to see how much work it has done to make me melanin god
a part of the night struggled away into oblivion, into the fights—
us against our green carpets, us against greenhouse gases.

The earth against our mistakes, call it the aftermath of raising what
would not want to see you stand. Call it ache, call it the encroaching
of all the hair I've managed to watch grow onto my scalp. Say, I'm
holding unto a storm in my left palm to protect my country
from this thing we have grown.

To blame the sun for—doom. I will blame my sons tomorrow
for not telling me a storm would always be a storm,
the way water would always create slow paths to drown
what it hates—earth.
I plant a flower in all the portholes our wrong steps have put on the road.

The roads have grown to home butterflies.
My brother is the first to see. My brother is a body of liquids—sea.
My brother is everything bent the wrong way—C.
My brother is a green covering of the earth—pea.
I have learned to live with a plant in my
right palm and a drought in my left palm. Call it adaptation, what must live [leave]

must learn to do it well—must survive [die]. In a small market
in *Sarkin Pawa*

there's a long term shift in temperatures—and weather pattern.
My people are too backwards to seek a weather forecast.
My people are too backwards to believe in rain
I have grown to know that nothing, ever beautiful, lasts forever

my people would wake on some days, the sun atop them foreheads
and watch
the clouds fade, watch the nights pull us into darkness.
There's a part of the earth
that is sinking, another is browning.
I watch every step I take towards green
pastures crack the earth and make way for skin breaks—
like my mothers lips

what remains of tenderness after the skin divides?
My fourth grandfather nurtured an oak tree,
my sister wants a beach house, so we take down the tree
we forsake the rules and put pillars in every spot that should home
a tree
the beach house stands erect in the absence of trees.
One day the earth would open and swallow its legs.
Nothing would dance to the rhythm of the wind

the wind starts a dry song from Kayes, across Cape Town,
through Nigeria
across the cracking of India, beyond Togo. The wind takes a lonely
path through my skin, through my people's homes, across all
the quiet places
that used to bed roses, call them graveyards. Every tree the wind

passes, bows and withers its leaves. Isn't this beauty?
Isn't this tenderness? Isn't this the time to gather the green we left

behind
put them in my people's palms, grow chad again into a beautiful garden?
I sit beneath what used to be a tree—there's an inferno of beautiful things

in my mouth, I spit them into all the wrong places,
the furrow on my accent
is louder than the storm that buried my home.
The night is becoming a hot
blanket atop my body, but I have learnt to be cold on hot days,
by catching my
breaths every time gases erupt. Like little prayers,
in the sanctuary of God.

10,000 BULLETS

Bello Abdullahi

A barren landscape stretches to the east and south, ending at a blank stucco wall to the north. To the west, close to the epicenter, a gigantic castle rises into the firmament. The castle's firm fibers provide a solid foundation, like the Pyrenees, dotted with plump bricks. The baked bricks stick out intermittently like desert dunes. Climbing up and down the bricks is a new wave of attention-grabbing creatures—the black monsters.

The monsters, though few, crawl up and down the castle tirelessly. They have horns and thorns, large heads with compound eyes, and powerful jaws. They appear to have six legs, each with three joints and spikes protruding from a body that looks like a black exoskeleton. Their red eyes and jaws trigger chills, but their actions show no sign of danger. No groans emerge from them. The climbers mind their own business and quietly make their way to the top of the castle—multiple facades extending into space.

But are they harmless? Well, that remains to be seen. A turn of events is needed to see how these creatures react with the ecosystem, and perhaps, one may draw conclusions from their actions.

Then, in an inexplicable direct response to this wonderment, the castle shakes as if hit by an earthquake. Actually, it's the work of an invisible force that strikes without warning and only manages to cause a slight shake. A few of the black monsters, however, lose their balance and topple over. As a matter of urgency, they sprint to the top, looking for sanctuary. Raucous laughter sounds from above—the work of an invisible, barbaric god.

From the look of things, these creatures are harmless peasants, gallivanting around, looking for food, scared of the invisible force and laughter. But who dares defy god? Perhaps the best way to conclude is to see how the black monsters host their peers or species of a lesser pedigree.

As if in response to the wonderment, once again, a dinosaur drops from the sky. The drop occurs some paces off to the east. It's a dead creature with bloodshot eyes, four legs, and claws. Is it the invincible god playing games? Or is this manna from heaven? Again, that remains to be seen.

The black monsters have retired into the castle, thanks to the invisible force. Up north, however, a lone wanderer emerges from the confines of the stucco wall and heads for the castle. This one's lucky to have missed the invisible force by minutes. It scuttles across the vast terrain, unmindful of the open heat. Then it notices—or rather, smells—the prey. Almost instantly, it changes direction.

As the predator approaches its prey, it extends two sharp incisors that resemble sickles. It hesitates for a moment, perhaps to smell more of its victims or to take a moment to prepare before launching an attack. Eventually, it decides to strike, slashing into the carcass and using its incisors to rip it apart. Groans emanate from the body, but the hunter does not devour its meal. Instead, it goes on a mission to displace its target. Unfortunately, the physics of force and motion are not on the ravager's side, as the target is almost fifty times larger than the predator itself. Despite several attempts, the hunter fails to accomplish its mission and ultimately abandons the remains, darting off into the castle.

Not long after that, a constellation of black monsters spills from the castle. They ultimately crowd around the fallen prey and drag it back toward the habitat. Certainly, a co-conspiracy has been involved. Judging by the way the creatures pour out—in thousands—the newfound brunch must be a special dish in their world. Unfortunately, they can't make it halfway to the castle. They are hit by bullets from above.

Rat-ta-ta-ta-ta-ta…, goes the sound. One by one, they fall. The bullets seem to descend from a military tank hanging in the sky above and moving along with precision. Invisible bullets from the sky? A hanging military tank? It must be the work of that barbaric god. For sure. But why does he want to exterminate the black monsters? Monsters are monsters, anyway.

The sound of gunfire continues without pause, and the black monsters fall in droves. Realizing they are under attack, they abandon their meal and flee for their lives toward the safety of the castle.

"Run!" some of them shout. "We're under attack!"

Unfortunately, many of them do not make it, even to the foot of the castle, and collide with a sudden surge of water from the southerly wing. Some drown in the deluge, while others...

"Denge," a loud voice booms, interrupting. "Come here."

That's my mother calling me. Game over.

Nothing ruins a day more than being interrupted in the middle of a game of 10,000 Bullets, a fun game where you kill live ants as they emerge from their habitat. You don't need a computer or a PlayStation for this game. I often start by deciding on the number of bullets—usually set at 10,000—and count my kills afterward. The more dead ants, the higher the points. To get the ants out of their habitat, I set a trap.

"Denge," my mother calls again. "Get away from that tree."

I'm tempted to take one last look at the spot. A few of the ants have regrouped, likely planning to make another attempt at the brunch.

"I'll be back, you sons of bitches," I yell at them.

Before I go to my mom, I should tell you a bit about myself. My name is Denge Sabo, and at age 10, I am the world's greatest ant killer. I am the barbaric god.

We live in Gembu, a quaint town in Northeastern Nigeria known for its rolling green hills, mini-forests and a plethora of white-washed bungalows with weathered roofs. A thriving metropolis for ants and bees. The townsfolk do not take pride in this unique coexistence, and this is why.

Every spring, a gazillion bees migrate in a massive, buzzing swarm. They usually don't go far, clustering on a nearby tree branch or wooded structure. Then they begin the business of establishing their new colony and making sweet, sweet honey. *Mmm!* I love them bees. But don't get me wrong. They sometimes sting. The ants, on the other hand, are a great nuisance. They burrow our most valued treasure, invade our food closets, and sting anyone standing in their way—even babies in their cradles.

Surely, someone needs to do the cleansing.

"Denge!"

Oops! My mother calls again. I'll be back in a jiffy.

I left the habitation of the ants scratching my head vigorously. A new wave of black monsters had taken over my scalp, and I could feel them crawling around on my skull, causing a severe itching sensation. I wanted to pull off my hair, scratch them, and teach them a lesson. Perhaps I could crush them with my knotty fingers or throw them off my head and stamp them under my feet. But the ants were well placed to be exposed to my aggressions, and they were driving me crazy.

I found Mother sitting in a cluster on the veranda, and Aunt Beshin held a can of insect spray. Scribbled on it, in bold, italicized fonts, was the word *Sheltox*. They looked at me expectantly as I crossed the lawn to the veranda. Per routine, I sat on a mini stool and placed my head on Mother's lap.

"How are you feeling?" Mother asked.

"They are still walking around in my head." My way of saying *not fine*. Even as I said this, I scratched.

"Don't worry," she consoled. "Your aunt just brought in a new insect spray. It's called Sheltox. It's deadlier than the others. By the grace of God, after two or three sprays, it'll get rid of all the lice roaming on your head."

Her words gave me hope. I looked up at the tin spray, following the descriptive word meticulously. I was so engulfed in trying to get the full details that I forgot about the routine of the moment.

"Put your head down, boy." Aunt Beshin's words brought me back.

First, Mother put on gloves and washed my hair with soap and water. She sped up the drying process by jamming my head under the blow dryer. Then Aunt Beshin went to work with the insect spray. She splashed the Sheltox on the mound of black hair, caressing every part with her gloved fingers to ensure it penetrated deep into the skull. I felt a slight burning sensation as the chemical made contact with the skin, likewise the lice receded into the safety of the thick hair strands.

Done with the spray, Beshin packed her things and left. Mother, too, retired into the inner sanctum for late-morning chores. I was left alone on the veranda, feeling refreshed. I weighed my chances. The game of 10,000 Bullets was not over yet. I still had to diffuse a few thousand bullets to hit the target. But going back for the second round of the game would demand extreme measures. I'd have to be cagey about it. Usually, after every spray, I was supposed to sit on the veranda for the next hour to allow the chemical to dry up. To me, that's a waste of game time, so I snuck through the back to the lone pineapple tree, wherein lay the dead baby-lizard and my weapons.

The ants swarmed in their multitudes. My absence sparked their audacity to come out in such sheer numbers. They succeeded in causing a slight displacement of the lizard, but were nowhere near the tree.

I studied the environment further before embarking on the kill. I could envisage having the greatest fun of my life killing all those black monsters. Nothing or no one could stand in my path right now, provided Mother and Aunt Beshin kept their distances.

I stooped low to pick up my weapons: a can of bug spray and a hard-soled sandal. As I stood up, I saw it. It hovered in front of my eyes. Wings flapped, buzzing incessantly like a vibrating cell phone. I was instantly drawn to it, not just by the buzzing sound, but also by the yellow-and-black stripes—my favorite colors.

I'm bringing home a baby bumblebee,
Won't my mommy be so proud of me…

I sang merrily, admiring the insect in front of me and, at the same time, wishing for it to go away. But it didn't. It darted to the left, then to the right, before sticking to my left earlobe. I tried to swat it away with my hand and partially succeeded, but it flew to my right ear lobe instead. By now, the buzzing intensified, and I became annoyed.

"Get off me, you stupid thing," I said, flapping my ear lobes to get rid of it, but I was too late. It stung me. The pain shot through my head like a thousand needles. I was so angry I crushed the bee against my cheeks, slapping myself in the process. The bee sting and the sharp pain from the slap created a ringing sensation in my ears.

"Ouch!" I crouched low to regain my composure, dropping my weapons and burying my head in my arms. It took a while for the pain to subside and the ringing to stop.

I took a deep breath and stood up. One small nuisance out of the way. Time to get on with the game. But I was wrong. A couple of bees, then two or three more, appeared out of nowhere and battled for control of my face. I flapped at them continuously, trying to shoo them away, but it was no use. They kept coming back. Their incessant buzzing was driving me crazy, so I crushed them, just like the previous one, by clapping my hands in the space they occupied. But they were too fast for me. They zigzagged, changing positions every two seconds. My failures turned to anxiety, and then to frustration.

Madness set in. I hit them with a frequency beyond my comprehension. The bees saw the danger and zeroed in on my face. Then the real stings began. One bee bit the nape of my neck. I crushed it without even realizing it. Another bee ripped off a piece of my upper lip and got away with it. The third one tried to get at my eyeballs, but it nipped my eyelids instead. I smashed it, along with my eyes. My vision exploded with a blinding flash. In the ensuing frenzy, I stepped on slippery ground and fell on my back with a thud. The impact knocked the breath out of me. I lay still, eyes closed, working to catch my breath. The blinding flash gave way to darkness.

I opened my eyes to blurred vision, which gradually cleared. I grew thoroughly exhausted. The fall dislodged parts of the dead lizard, scattering ants over a large area. I took another breath and rose to my feet.

Bumble bees!

My heart sank at the sight of them, as there were too many to count. They rushed at me as if I were a flower.

Something was wrong. Something was terribly wrong.

I made the final decision to terminate the game for the time being, since the bees turned trigger-happy for reasons best known to them. I could resume the game of 10,000 Bullets when the bees returned safely back to their hives.

Once again, I acted too late. Dozens of bees crowded around my head, sending me scampering for cover. Regrettably, there was no place to hide in the big backyard, which had nothing in it except the pineapple tree, a.k.a., the castle of the black monsters. Down below, the neighboring houses looked inviting. They were bungalows of the same make and the same backyard, bearing a pineapple tree or trees in some cases, a mark for all public housing projects. However, I quickly decided against it. I would not be laughed at by my friends for barging into their houses with bees swarming, screaming for help.

With so many attacking bees, it was difficult to focus. Somehow, I thought of my mother, and my mind settled on what to do next. I scuttled across the lawn to the main courtyard, then stopped dead in my tracks. Bees swarmed over the courtyard, occupying every breathing space. I never saw so many insects in my life.

"Mummy!" I screamed. "Help! Mummy, please help me!"

The call for help was answered immediately. Mother came rushing out of the house, her head covered in a white shawl. She grabbed my hand and dragged me across the veranda into the lounge as Aunt Beshin locked the door behind her. A small pack of bees made it into the room as well. Considering they were not of colossal amount, Aunt Beshin had a field day crushing them.

I was saved for the time being, but that did not reflect on my face because a gazillion others remained outside. There was so much buzzing. We beheld the mounting tragedy from the glass windows, whose shutters fit tightly to prevent any leak. I refused to go closer when the bees began to pound on the glass and window panes, trying to find their way in. When they couldn't gain entry, they switched over to the door and attained some degree of success. In response, Aunt Beshin and Mother quickly rammed pieces of clothes into the tiny pores at the edges. Not even air could leak out.

I felt safe once more. But the sights and sounds outside the house strongly interrupted that feeling. How could you be safe with all those creatures flying around? *No, we aren't safe. Not until those insects leave our compound.*

"Oh, Lord!" Mother exclaimed. "Bear us from this adversity." From the look on her face, she was scared, too.

"Where are they from?" Aunt Beshin asked.

"Search me." Mother crossed her arms.

"I have never seen anything like this," Aunt Beshin went on.

"Me neither."

Mother looked at me, and her expression changed. "Oh, my God! Look at what they did to your face!"

I crossed to a standing mirror and gazed upon myself for the first time since being attacked. I looked like a battered case: face ashen and wet with sweat; eyes and lips swollen.

"I think we're in deep trouble," Aunt Beshin said urgently, jolting me out of my thoughts. She excused herself to use the bathroom and emerged, looking horrified.

"What's going on?" Mother asked, just as perplexed.

"They've made their way into the bathroom."

We all rushed to see for ourselves, and our blood ran cold. So focused on blocking the bees from the living room, we forgot to close the windows in the other rooms. The situation in the bedroom got worse. Little Adama and Asma'u began to cry on the bed. We managed to free them from the grasp of the deadly insects.

"We need to get out of the house," Mother warned, locking the bedroom door.

"How?" Beshin asked. "We're surrounded."

Mother fell silent.

Then relief came in the form of a voice calling out to us. Looking through the window, I saw my father with a man in dark blue jeans and a short, brown caftan. The man held a burnt-out tree branch, billowing with smoke. Dad covered his head with a piece of plastic. Despite the bee swarm, the two men made their way to the veranda.

Father ordered us to leave the house, which we did. Sandwiched between him and the man in the blue jeans, we hurried to our Range Rover parked out front. The driver was in position, waiting patiently. Mother, Aunt Beshin, and the two girls squeezed into the back seat. Abubakar and Abdulrahman sat comfortably in the front. As I moved to join them, a swarm of bees landed on me. The weight was so heavy and sudden my father and the man in the blue jeans had to retreat. That's when I realized—I was their target.

The bees clung to me from head to toe, turning me into a mummified hive. Dad and the man in the blue jeans did their best to rid me of the vile insects but failed. The stings kept coming, and my body felt as though it were on fire.

I lost my mind.

I ran, screaming at the top of my lungs, without regard for direction. The sprint helped shake the bees off me. I headed toward the mini-forest with the pond. No part of the neighborhood had been spared. As far as I could see, bees occupied all breathing space.

Gazillions of them buzzed incessantly, attacking whoever—or whatever—was unfortunate enough to stand in their path.

I spotted families taking off in their Range Rovers, unable to bear the blitz. The brave ones remained locked indoors, hoping the tragic incident would subside naturally. Some called out for me to seek refuge in their homes, but my mind was spinning. I didn't stop until I reached the pond in the woods, where I dove in with a splash.

The bees retired to their nests at dusk, and that night beekeepers invaded every home with the sole aim of driving bees out and using smoke to extract honeycombs. The man in the dark blue jeans was one of them.

After the honeycombs were tapped, he cornered me in a section of the house for a chat. He explained he found me in the pond. He believed the insect spray on my head stirred the bees, as they hate the smell of insecticides. Then he subjected me to a flurry of questions to quench his suspicion.

"What sort of game were you playing?" he asked.

"10,000 Bullets," I replied.

"Describe it."

"I have to kill as many ants as possible with 10,000 bullets."

"Did you?"

"No."

"Why?"

"Mother and Aunt Beshin interrupted the game. They had to shampoo my head with Sheltox."

"What happened after that?"

"The bees came."

The man considered this for a bit and then said, "Did you learn your lesson?"

I nodded. "The bees hate Sheltox. Never go near them when you are scented."

"Ants and bees are great co-conspirators, boy. Remember that," he said. "If they were humans, they could topple governments with their mass action."

Imagine that! Ants and bees allied. From that day, I did not rule out the possibility of a collaboration between the ants and the bees to get rid of me—for good.

FEAR

Section 3

IMPEDIMENTA

Charmaine Denison-George

We traveled light, without bags. Host brother and I wore sweatshirts, which we later tied around our hips under the sweltering sun. Our sunglasses slung back on the top of our heads; cell phones, earphones, and cardholders in our jean pockets. Host dad arranged the round-trip flight from Pune to Agra via New Delhi and wrote a note of absence for my host brother's high school, an hour away from mine. He reasoned I could not, as a seventeen-year-old West African girl, travel to New Delhi unaccompanied. I had no issues with these terms as it meant that I, like my classmates whose spring breaks included the beaches of Goa or snow-capped mountains in Ladakh, could post splendid photos on my Instagram feed of the Taj Mahal.

As we exited the ticketing office in Agra, a young and burly tour guide (with a name I do not recall) flagged us down. For payment, he asked for "something small plus tip." Moments later, we were headed toward an archway of red and white that led to the Taj Mahal Gardens.

I contemplated using the bathroom, which I remembered to be off in a corner, somewhere between the ticketing office and the gate. Host brother discouraged the thought, saying he imagined a long queue, and the tour guide mused it would be a shame to come so far to miss the sunrise on the Taj Mahal. So, I silently moved along.

The historic landmark was a vision set in blush, red, and gold. I was rendered speechless as a gentle breeze enticed us from the gate into the gardens. A few people gasped at the sight as our tour guide spewed facts about the grounds: the 22 years of construction signified by the 11 minarets on both sides of the gate; the view from the nearby Agra fort; the architecture of the Taj Mahal itself—a Shah's ode to a deceased wife, an expensive manifestation of true love.

I considered the bilateral symmetry, how carefully the gardens and the pools of water were constructed. Then we perused the landing of the mausoleum, tucking our phones away in our pockets. We wore the filmy covers over our tennis shoes, and all the while, I thought, *I should have used the bathroom before coming this far.*

Just a few weeks before my trip to Agra, I was introduced to Leslee Udwin's documentary, *India's Daughter*. The film followed the 2012 rape case of a young woman since dubbed "Nirbhaya" or "India's daughter." The 23-year-old was brutally assaulted in a moving bus and left for dead on the streets of Delhi. I was incensed by the interviewed men who confessed to raping her that night and the bus driver who suggested she should have just stayed put while being raped. And so, by recency and Delhi proximity, I kept thinking about the film. I had not known, as I now know, about fearful overthinking—how it is a day's job of its own, how it impedes clarity.

So, as I trod off from my host brother and tour guide, looking for the bathroom, the film came to mind. There was a long queue, and I waited my turn for a stall. When my wait was over, it seemed business as usual until I was done and noticed I could not get out of the toilet's closet.

I tugged at the door handle, but to no avail. I was caged in. A nauseating dread overtook me. I would meet my demise in Delhi! I shook the door and screamed, begging to be let out. Will no one respond to my calamity? Had those ladies in the queue all been in on a wicked scheme to end me?

After a few moments, I looked down and spotted the door latch I had shut minutes prior. Good sense had finally reared its head, and I unhooked the door, emerging from the toilet shaking with a scratchy throat. In the eternity that it took to wash my hands at the basin (while averting my eyes from meeting the eyes of others), I felt as Gabriella Montez of *High School Musical* once said: "humiliated into the next century."

FROM SACRED LANDS TO FRAGILE SEAS

Tiara Imani Blain

Will you ever get out of the water?" Toran asks. "We have the rest of Lagos to see."

"Sorry," Ashanti tells Toran in a playful tone. "I have a hard time leaving the water. I'm drawn to it."

"Babe, you have ancestors who once walked this land. You'll be drawn to many places here, but we'll never see them if you float in the water all day."

"There's something about being here in particular, connecting with our roots."

"Yeah," Toran agrees. "And your mom tried her best to talk us out of coming here for our honeymoon."

"She did." Ashanti mimics her mother in a mocking tone. "*Why do you want to go there for your honeymoon? Don't be out too late at night.* She's constantly worrying. She means well, but she overwhelms me with her fear."

Toran laughs. "That does sound like her." He then nudges Ashanti again. "So, how long *are* you going to stay in the water?"

"Fine, fine," Ashanti says. "Let's go."

She glances back at the ocean. It is clear as crystal, revealing the gray and brown rocks of the sea floor. Ashanti wonders about the water—its history. *What exactly did it experience? What did it see?* As she moves her eyes toward the Atlantic, the water suddenly becomes a bright red, as if mixed with blood. Ashanti shakes her head as though to toss out the image.

"You okay?" Toran asks.

"I don't think so," Ashanti says, her eyes dancing in panic. "Red water—blood… I feel like I'm losing it."

"It's okay," Toran attempts to calm her, "Breathe—breathe."

Ashanti inhales deeply, then slowly until the panic disappears from her eyes.

"You feel so deeply, Shanti," Toran comforts. "Are you imagining what has happened here—in these waters?"

Ashanti laughs to herself. *Why does he know me so well?* From the beginning of their relationship, Toran knew how to deal with her struggles, her anxiety disorder, her anxiety attacks, her fixating thoughts. Ashanti takes a deep breath. *That's why I married him.*

"I will not let my anxiety ruin our honeymoon," she says, as if trying to convince herself as well as her husband. "I know that sometimes I can get stuck on things, and worrisome like my mom—"

"It's okay, babe," Toran reassures her. "Trust me, this is going to be an experience of a lifetime."

It had been a long day of sightseeing. Ashanti and Toran end the day lying in the hammock outside of their vacation villa. Ashanti looks over to see Toran asleep and smiles. *With a view like this, of course, he would be asleep.*

The multitude of stars create diamond-like glimmers in the navy-blue water. Ashanti watches the diamonds sparkle like magic. *This doesn't compare to anything I have seen in Charlotte.* She decides she will enjoy every bit of it before they return to their everyday lives in North Carolina.

Ashanti's train of thought grows sour. She reflects on what she knows of the Atlantic Slave Trade. *How could people take others from their home?* She can't even imagine what her ancestors faced. Her eyes grow weary, beginning to close right before she notices a dark blue figure surrounding a large wave. Ashanti's eyes open wide before the figure disappears. She sits up in the hammock. *What was that?*

Ashanti looks over at Toran, who rests in a blissful slumber. She doesn't want to wake him. *It must have been a reflection in the water*, she thinks. And soon after, Ashanti falls into a deep sleep, too.

Ashanti awakes to find herself back at the beach at night. She stands in shallow water, where the sand meets the ocean. Something cold and hard brushes at her feet. She looks down to see broken shackles. She picks up and examines the rusted chains before dropping them in front of a blue figure, then clearly a brown face.

The woman wears large black braids that fall past her waist. She doesn't resemble anyone Ashanti has ever seen. She radiates an indescribable beauty, glowing skin, and angelic brown eyes. When Ashanti looks down at the clear water, she sees the creature has an iridescent fin. It doesn't frighten Ashanti as things usually do. She surprisingly feels comfort, as if she were one with the woman-like creature.

"Who are you?" Ashanti asks, staring into eyes that glimmered with the sea.

"I go by many names."

The creature speaks in Yoruba, but Ashanti somehow understands, as if the communication is spirit to spirit.

A hand reaches for her, the palm and wrist covered in jewels. Ashanti drifts her hand towards it. As the hands join, she feels a powerful force generate throughout her body. Ashanti herself forms scales and a fin. Her hair, already in braids, grows as long as the woman's.

The two suddenly sink into the ocean, zooming through water at lightning speed. They travel deeper and deeper into the depths of the sea, further than all who have tried and failed. Swiftly, they pass sea creatures Ashanti never knew existed. The two pierce through a protective layer, resembling diamond glass into what seems to be an underwater island. The sphere-like shape reflects hues of blue, purple, and pink, complementing the exotic fruits on the island trees. The air smells like shea, pine, and honey. The two women land on a seafloor. The sand feels stiff, yet soft as shea butter. Once they hit dry land, their fins transform into feet.

Both women walk among an island of merpeople. Men and women dressed in extravagant tribal attire. Their skin, as smooth as silk in multiple shades of brown, tan, and beige. They appear to have scales similar to hers.

Overwhelmed with emotion, Ashanti asks the woman, "Who are they?"

The woman looks at Ashanti, then back at the others. "They're the ones who took to the sea."

Ashanti suddenly awakens in the hammock.

Toran is up and about. He walks in from the bathroom. "I found an area nearby I think we'll like. Come, let's go."

"Wait a moment," Ashanti groans, still taken aback by last night's dream and unable to hide her crankiness at Toran's push to get her up. "Fine. I will get ready soon."

As the couple walk hand in hand down the street, Ashanti notices a book in the window of a bookstore. An image of an African mermaid sits on the cover, one like the woman in her dream. The title reads *Yemaya, The Sea Goddess.*

Ashanti wastes no time. She rushes into the store, grabs the book, and asks the guy behind the counter, "Do you have other books about this sea goddess?"

"Only this one," he replies.

Excitedly, Ashanti takes the book to the sitting area and shares with Toran about the night before.

"I dreamt about this mermaid last night!" she says, flipping through the pages, gobbling as much info as she can in a short time. "So, what I am getting from this book is that Yemaya is a mermaid in Yorubian folklore. She is considered a goddess and mother of the ocean."

"That's dope," says Toran.

"The book has the history of the folktale, but none of this helps with what the dream meant."

Ashanti turns to her phone to research more. "Ugh. Google gives the same information." She slouches, props elbows on her knees, and cups her face in her hands.

A local woman passes by, noticing the cover of the book. "Oh, you're reading about the African mermaid, Yemaya!"

Ashanti lifts her eyes to see a woman with black and dark blonde cornrowed hair, beads at the end of each braid. "My grand-aunt would always mention the story of Yemaya when I was a child."

"Really?" Ashanti replies. "Are you able to tell me more about her?"

"Well, I don't remember much," the woman says.

Ashanti's head lowers in disappointment.

The woman shows pity. "You know what, if you are not busy right now, and you want to know more, my aunt only lives a couple of blocks away. I will call her now to see if she is up to meeting with you."

"I would love that!" Ashanti brightens. "Thank you. I'm Ashanti, by the way, and this is my husband, Toran."

"It's nice to meet you both," the woman says. "My name is Yara."

Yara calls her aunt, while Toran takes Ashanti to the side.

"Babe, we can't go to a stranger's house in another country. I would think you, of all people, wouldn't be comfortable with this."

"But Toran, I have to figure this out," Ashanti replies. "Something is telling me I need to know more. This is happening for a reason."

"I don't know, this is crazy," Toran says.

Overhearing some of their conversation, Yara interjects, "You don't have to worry. It's a busy street. We can talk on the patio outside the house."

Ashanti looks at Toran with a pleading, pouted face.

"Okay, okay," he says, "We can check it out. But if I feel any concerns, we're out of there."

Ashanti gives him a big smile and a peck on the lips. "Thank you, babe!"

They all walk to Yara's aunt's house, not too far from the bookstore. As they arrive, they see the older woman sitting on the front yard porch, dressed in a traditional wrap with matching headdress, patterned in a red, yellow, blue, and black. She is short and stout in stature, yet gives off a bold presence.

The elderly aunt rises and greets everyone with a welcoming smile.

Yara bows, touches her foot, and says, "*e kaaro*, Aunty Adola. Good morning."

Her aunt gestures for her to stand. "Good morning, child," she says. "Are these the friends you've told me about?"

"Yes, this is Ashanti and Toran," Yara replies. They are traveling from America and wanted to learn more about Yemaya."

Toran and Ashanti greet Aunty Andola with a slight bow.

"Thank you so much for having us," Ashanti says. "You don't know how grateful I am to meet with you."

"No worries, child. An old woman like me is happy to have the company."

Ashanti, Toran, and Yara sit on the porch stoop around Miss Adola who returns to her seat in a woven rocking chair. The woman closes her eyes for a moment, rocking back and forth. Then she slowly opens her eyes.

"Yemaya is the goddess and mother of the ocean," Miss Adola says. "She is also the mother of fertility and healing. She guides the women and protects the people. She's the eldest daughter of *Olodumare*."

"*Olodumare*?" Ashanti ask

"Yes," Adola explains, "the one who spreads virtue and morality. Just one of the three manifestations of God, the creator of Heaven and Earth. *Olorun* is the ruler of the heavens, and *Olofi* is the link between Heaven and Earth. Yemaya—she watches over the ocean and all that lives therein.

"As the goddess of the ocean, Yemaya bore witness to the fate of the enslaved who were taken to the New World. She comforted and protected them during the Atlantic Slave Trade. Her story traveled with the people throughout America, the Caribbean islands, and other Afro-Latino cultures.

"People say she helped those who jumped in the water, taking them to land, sometimes returning them to the boat. My grandmother would tell me about her grandfather, who fell from a boat during the transatlantic trade. A 50-foot wave surrounding a blue figure carried him back to the land. The nearby villages heard the story. Some spoke of similar experiences. Others thought the story was a fable, but most needed the hope Yemaya brought.

"She was a symbol of our hope. A few even believed there were still Africans alive down there. These souls are the ones that took to the sea."

Ashanti remembered the underwater island in her dreams. "Like merpeople?"

Adola nodded. "It is but a rumor that some have been visited by Yemaya and taken to this place. So, we have those looking after us from beneath the seas *and* above the heavens."

Before Yara could ask another question, an alert pings on Yara's phone. "Oh, I'm so sorry. I totally forgot I have to take Aunty to her doctor's appointment."

"Oh, no worries."

"It was a pleasure meeting you both," Yara says. "Please take my number. Let me know if you want to get together before you travel back home."

"We will. Thank you."

Miss Adola rises once again to bid the couple farewell, "*O Dabo* Miss Adola says, "Goodbye."

"O Dabo," says Ashanti and Toran. Ashanti also hugs Yara in gratitude.

The honeymooners take a taxi to the beach. They sit, watching the waves roll in and listening to the water's soft groan.

"I still don't really understand why I am having these dreams," Ashanti says, resting her head on Toran's thigh.

Toran gently plays with her curls. "Maybe your ancestors are trying to tell you something."

Ashanti scoffs, "Me, the anxious one?"

"Well, it doesn't seem coincidental," Toran says. "Something is connecting you to all of this. Of all places, we chose Nigeria to celebrate our union. And you heard what Miss Adola said. People claim to have seen this underwater city. You are not the only one."

Ashanti sighs, "Maybe you're right."

Weary from the day, Ashanti and Toran lie down on the blanket and hold one another. She listens to the sea's comforting roar and dozes off.

Ashanti suddenly rises with the mermaid in the exact spot she had been the night before. *What is going on*? she says to herself.

Ashanti turns to the goddess. "Yemaya? You're Yemaya, aren't you?"

Yemaya nods, then turns around, walking towards a sunken pit in the seafloor. Ashanti follows behind.

"I was there when it all happened," says Yemaya. "The slave trade. I heard the noise of it, the whips, the cries, the screams. I heard it all. What I saw was horrific. How people could be so cruel."

Yemaya's voice cracks as she holds back tears. "Centuries later, I still feel every plea, every desperate expression. None of us should forget what happened."

Ashanti tears up, witnessing Yemaya's pain.

Yemaya leans over the hole, gesturing for Ashanti to do the same.

"What is this?" Ashanti asks.

"This is all that's left," Yemaya says.

They look to see the debris of old spears, whips, and tarnished strips of cloth. There are rusted shackles and chains, just like the shackles Ashanti had found in the water the night before. Suddenly the items vanish, and the hole fills with water.

"When I heard the screams of those plowing into the water, I did what I could to help, but the bodies plummeted so quickly. Those I couldn't rescue, I brought to a life below the sea on this island. *Ogo ni fun Olorun, baba mi.* Glory be to God, my father.

"I could protect them and keep them alive. These have been with me ever since and will be until the world's end. They don't age. They don't die, but they can never return to the surface.

"Few get to see this island or know we exist," Yemaya explains. "Only those who need to know. This island is just for us."

"This is so amazing," Ashanti says, looking at the paradise. "But I still don't understand. Why show all of this to me?"

"I brought you here because there are some things you must know," says Yemaya.

"Yes?"

Yemaya takes a deep breath. "There is a curse in your family's bloodline."

"A curse?" Ashanti grows alarmed. "What do you mean by a curse? Like a trans-generational curse?"

"That's exactly what I mean," Yemaya replies. "Your great-great-great grandmother's parents were of those who leapt from the boat." Yemaya points across the island to a man and woman. "Do you see them?"

Ashanti notices the young couple from afar. "I see them!"

"Well, when I came to the surface, seeing their ship in the distance, I found Ayoola floating in the ocean. A toddler, about 3 years old. She was breathing."

"Ayoola?"

"Yes. I knew she had a purpose, a reason she had to be alive," Yemaya says. "She was destined to be on that boat, not in the sea."

Yemaya chuckles as though she remembers fondly. "I swam her back to the boat to sneak her back on. I knew someone would take care of her in the New World. She was to live a life on land."

"When Ayoola was 16 years of age, I came to her as I've to you. I told her I would help her lead an assembly of the enslaved to freedom. But Ayoola just couldn't do it, because of—fear."

Yemaya continues, "Ayoola feared that if she led the assembly, everyone would be killed. But it was her fear that led to the demise of everyone on the plantation, including herself. That fear has followed her generations until now."

Ashanti thinks about her own struggles with general anxiety disorder, her anxiety attacks, her fixating thoughts, her fears of crowds and social conflicts. She considers her mother's overprotectiveness borne of her own childhood secrets.

"Trauma immerses us in fear," Yemaya says, as though she reads Ashanti's mind. "After these years, someone must break this curse. That person is you."

Ashanti's lips part further and further until her jaw eventually drops. "Huh… how… what…" Gasping still, she eventually mutters a few words, "So… that was a lot."

Yemaya simply smiles and nods.

Ashanti continues, "I don't know. I can barely manage my anxiety, and I'm really supposed to end this curse for others?"

Yemaya wags an instructing finger. "A curse is often a person's greatest strength, only tested. Trusting your intuition to visit Miss Adola; having the courage to take my hand and come here. Now, that is bravery.

Allowing yourself to feel what your ancestors felt and what others feel—that's your superpower. This will help you as you nurture the next leader."

"The next leader?"

"Your daughter will lead a community of people to freedom."

"My what?" Ashanti interrupts. "Wait, I just got married. What's this talk about a daughter?"

"Listen," Yemaya tells her. "Your great-great-great grandmother wasn't up to the task, but your daughter will be because of you. You will break the curse of fear, the curse of holding onto pain and trauma. This will release your lineage from anxiety. You'll teach your daughter to speak up for herself, to be transparent, to be courageous.

"There was a reason I found Ayoola floating in the water, just like I found you floating the other day. There is power in your bloodline."

Ashanti stands in a daze and whispers, "My daughter." This time—it is not a question, but a statement.

Yemaya continues, "Your daughter will help lead many of African descent to freedom. So many are still emotionally and mentally enslaved. Some are even physically enslaved in our own homeland. It's time we heal. Our people have been drowning.

"The lost ones are not lost. It is the others who are suffocating in a world played against them, but it's time to breathe."

Yemaya fades from sight.

"Wait? But when?" Ashanti panics. "Can you tell me when my daughter is coming?"

As Yemaya fades, she smiles one last time. "*O ti wa ni bi ni sin.*"

A light beams on Ashanti's face.

"Ashanti? Ashanti?"

Disoriented, Ashanti rises to the sound of Toran's voice. She rushes to her phone to open the Google Translation app. She looks up Yemaya's last words, which, unlike the other times, she does not understand. "*O ti wa ni bi ni sin.*" When the app translates, she drops the phone.

Staring at the body of water before her, Ashanti repeats the translation as though in a trance, "She's already here."

BLUEBERRY PIE

Jody T. Pratt

Calvin tosses and turns on the twin-sized mattress, its springs sounding off in clanks and clinks. As he sits up, his shifting stomach acid makes his belly groan. He rubs it, reassuring that comfort will be on its way. Then, he plants his feet on the aged hardwood floor.

The floors creak and complain because of his heavy weight. Calvin stands upright into a teeth-chattering stretch. He pauses to not wake his grandparents, let alone his brother, whom occupies the same bed. His eldest brother sleeps soundly across the room. Having much practice, Calvin transfers weight from his heels to the tips of his toes.

He opens the door at a slug's pace and squeezes through it, but not past the point where the hinges would omit noise. His pacing pays off when he reaches the top of the staircase, staring down into a layer of darkness where there is a hint of moonlight. Behind a tightly fastened door, the hum of Grandpa Woods' sleep apnea machine slightly combats Grandma Odessa's stereo, which plays a melody of ocean waves and North American waterfalls.

Mr. Tum Tum, the family cat, bumps and nudges by, which reminds Calvin of his goal. As he descends the stairs, counting each step, Mr. Tum Tum blurts "meow" as if to tell his partner to hurry. Calvin places an index finger on his lips, then mouths a warning to the cat, *Imma eat yo' ass next.*

Heeding his warning, Mr. Tum Tum stretches before trotting the rest of the stairs to the source of the moonlight. Picking up the pace, Calvin floats down the rest of the way, cutting through the Georgia summer humidity that fills his grandparents' home.

Following the moonlight's length shown through the window above the sink, Calvin finds himself in the kitchen. A gurgling, flapping sound comes from his belly. One hand reaches for the handle of the old Wanderlust Co. fridge, while the other makes clockwise and counterclockwise motions around his belly. *So close to our reward.*

Pulling the handle slowly, Calvin hears the magnetic strip lining the frame *pop pap* and grows overzealous. He bites his lower lip and holds his breath as if it will help his anonymity. His hand falls from beneath his oversized "North Dakota Cougars" women's softball shirt to aid his other hand in opening the door.

The glorious, beige-tinted light illuminates the boy's smile and fills the kitchen. The refrigerator's engine sputters louder but is ignored by the door opener and Mr. Tum Tum who paws at the heavy whipping cream.

The young boy, who couldn't be older than 11 or 12, joins Mr. Tum Tum eagerly. He grabs grapes, a few tepid leftovers from dinner, swigs of milk, and orange juice labeled, "Grandma's Juice! Thieves will get the SWITCH!"

Calvin takes a bite and a half of all he sees, swallowing mouthfuls, making room for more. And there he saw it. Slightly hidden behind a half jug of whole milk, a fat slice of blueberry pie wrapped in cellophane on a small paper plate. No doubt in his mind, it was from last Wednesday's church service and fundraiser at Mercy's Touch Baptist

Church. The fundraiser, from what he and his brothers suspected, was for the pastor's new swimming pool.

Calvin gulps, only to make more room in his mouth. His crumb-covered smile grew as he reached with both hands towards the piece of pie.

"Calvin Lamont Westle? Boy, get yo' little ass up out my damn refrigerator! You done almost made me put you down, son!" says Grandpa Wood as he turns on the kitchen light.

Startled and embarrassed, Calvin bumps the back of his head exiting the refrigerator. His 71-year-old grandfather peers over the door, holding his matte, black .38 Special. The barrel is engraved with the words ON MY LAP AT ALL TIMES. Grandpa proceeds into the kitchen with bare feet, wearing a loose wife beater, form-fitting briefs, and his Marines *Semper Fi* tattoo dotted by patches of gray curls.

"So, this is what yo' momma and daddy was talkin' bout, huh?" Grandpa Wood fusses. "Comin' down at the devil's hour and eatin' all the damn food up! Have you been doing this all summer, boy?"

Calvin interrupts, trying to defuse being caught red-handed.

"No, Grandpa Wood, I… I… I heard something downstairs, and… and I came down to see what it was. The refrigerator was making weird noises and—"

"So, you decided to clean it out, son? Look at you. You covered in all sorts of junk—yesterday's sandwich, tonight's supper, and don't think I haven't noticed that extra pulp on your top lip."

Embarrassed, Calvin tries to hold on to some dignity, "I'm sorry, Grandpa. Please don't tell Mom and Da—"

Grandpa rolls his eyes, interjecting, "Boy, if I was a snitch, we would be in a mansion in a gated community, dammit."

Calvin laughs charitably, but feeding Grandpa's ego falls to the wayside this time. The old man's face goes deadpan.

"I ain't the one you gotta worry 'bout. It's somebody else you's got to worry about."

"Oh, you gon' tell Grandma?"

"Hush, boy! I'm talking 'bout Stumpy Johnson."

"Stumpy Johnston?"

"Johnson!" Grandpa shouts, "Never mind. Clean up and head on to the bed, boy."

Calvin agrees and washes his face in the lower-level bathroom. Grandpa Wood sweeps up the crumbs and wipes the droplets of juice to keep Grandma unaware.

Calvin peeks out of the bathroom door, turning off the light to be concealed in the darkness. He feels eyes on him, an unnerving stare in the opposite direction of the kitchen. Goosebumps spread from the back of his neck, down his spine, branching to his arms and legs. He turns only to see the darkness of the living room, confused at the wave of discomfort.

"Son, get yo' tail on to bed," Grandpa Wood interjects.

"I… I—" Calvin replies, pointing at the darkness of the living room. Grandpa, somewhat smiling and somewhat shaking his head, picks up his .38 from the counter. He moves toward the light switch, and Calvin scampers to the landing of the stairwell before he shuts them off.

As they start up the stairs, Grandpa Wood's free hand, damp from the sink rinse, lands on Calvin's shoulder.

"Look, son, you can't just eat 'cause you hungry. Let your body rest and let your mind relax. You want them boys to call you all them names forever?"

Calvin stares at his feet, climbing the stairs, defeated and embarrassed.

"I'm a take that as a *no*," Grandpa says. "They are your brothers, and they love you. You gotta stand up for yourself and not eat your feelings."

Calvin lets out a deep sigh. "I don't know. I get so hungry."

He picks up the speed on the last five steps, wanting the conversation to end. He stops before entering the room shared with his brothers over the last eight summers.

"Hey, Grampy?"

Grandpa answers winded, "Take yo' tail to bed, boy!"

Calvin pauses a few paces from his bedroom door, "Who is Stumpy Johnson?"

"Who?"

"S-Stumpy Johnson?"

"Ooh, yes, that's right!" Grandpa says, pivoting towards Calvin. "Let's see, Stumpy Johnson was an old and tattered house Negro on the Marie Plantation. That same one just over yonder by the creek. Skinny as the day is long, he was a mean-sum-bitch. Nasty too. He was so fair-skinned, he believed he was a white man when his master was gone. Dressing in his master's clothes, sleeping in the master's bed. Whenever the master leaves the plantation from business or what have you. Until he was caught sleeping in the master's bed. Mmm, boy was beaten so bad he ended up losing his left arm from the elbow down due to infection. And they tried to take his foot, but he pleaded and begged, promising he would forever be beholden of 'Massa.' And halfway through cutting it off, they stopped. So now, you can hear him walk through the night with a *thump—slide, thump—slide.*

"He paid the price for overstepping in front of all the slaves. He was sent from living in the main house to living in the basement, only to come out at night and do his work. To make it up to his master, he would carry around an unfinished wooden club whittled from an oak tree. He'd say, 'I'm trying to catch the youngin's making mischief and stealing food.'

"Stumpy Johnson took joy in the catch—and even more in the punishment. He would leave out food sometimes—just for kicks. He would even sing a little song... like... erm… oh:

Greedy, Greedy little Negro
Using the night for one's own plunder
Greedy, Greedy little Negro
Let this club cure your hunger.
Greedy, Greedy little Negro
Eating Massa out of house and home
Greedy, Greedy little Negro."

Calvin cringes at the song. The hair on the back of his neck stands tall.

Grandpa further explains, "As Stumpy sings his tune, your body freezes in horror as his strides are slow. Before you know it, your hand is glued to the nearest surface. Your eyes are unblinking, unmoving, no matter how much your heart desires. He raises his club high into the darkness, then—THWHACK!" Grandpa Wood claps his hand in Calvin's face, making him flinch and step back. Stunned, Calvin's heart thumps hard in his chest.

"Welp, gon' head to bed now, boy," says Grandpa, shutting off the hallway light with the muzzle of his .38.

Calvin stands speechless. Consumed by the night, he quickly retreats into his shared room. He feels as if those staring eyes are still at the bottom of the stairwell. He slams his bedroom door quickly behind him, which, surprisingly, leaves the room unbothered. The silence gives him a sense of relief. He takes a few steps backward until his heel catches a Hot Wheel, causing him to lose balance. One arm braces for landing, and the other shoots out towards his older brother's bed with no clear grip. Calvin lands on his bottom with a bounce. He closes his eyes and stifles a groan for the sake of the room.

Pausing in embarrassment, Calvin hears a voice, ever so slightly, downstairs. One that labors to breathe.

"Ha-ha, you didn't hurt yourself now, did yah? Greedy, greedy little Negro?"

Calvin opens his eyes in confusion. *Nah, Grandpa Wood wouldn't go this far to scare me just because I ate the rest of the roast beef and grapes.*

Faint thumps ascend the staircase. He scrambles and leaps to the full-sized bed shared with his older brother, Kevin.

"Calvin, you need to chill," Kevin says, turning over to find slumber again.

"Did you hear that, Kevin?" Calvin asks, pulling the covers over himself.

Kevin fails to respond. Calvin realizes Kevin doesn't have his hearing aid in. *That can't be Stumpy Johnson. He... He's not real. He can't be real.*

The slow thumps become heavier and less rhythmic. *Thump—thump——thump-thump.*

Calvin pulls the covers over his head.

A fusty odor of rot wafts through the dense humid air. An aroma that Calvin can taste, replacing the dollar store Wild Mint Madness toothpaste applied earlier. Calvin can no longer manage his breath. He closes his eyes, muttering words of comfort, images of home, love, and happiness from his parents.

The thumps come to a sudden halt, and Calvin's eyes peer from beneath the frayed Snoopy cover. He looks around the room and finds nothing out of the ordinary. A sudden movement brings his attention to the two-inch space at the bottom of the door and the aged hardwood floor. He sits on his knees in wonderment, trying to comprehend the situation. Outside the door, a pair of what seems to be decaying feet stands, leaving Calvin at a loss for words. Tears flow as he grips his covers. There's a slight turn of the door knob.

Greedy, Greedy little Negro
Using the night for one's own plunder
Greedy, Greedy little Negro
Let this club cure—

Shaking in dread, Calvin lets out a scream, trying to alert his older brothers. Andre partially sits up in response. Calvin points to the bottom of the bedroom door where he sees the shadow. He screams.

"Andre! Kevin! It's Stumpy Johnson!"

Calvin leaps from his bed with fists clenched tight. The door handle turns ever so slightly. Andre sends a pillow hurling at his youngest brother's head. The show of force to suggest, *Calvin, shut up*!

Calvin runs to the door, applying his entire body weight against it. He then grasps the door handle with all his strength, but he can hardly stop the movement. The odor intensifies to the point Calvin retches repeatedly. The sound arouses Andre in a fury.

"Calvin, what the hell are you doing? What is that smell?"

"H-help me! It's Stumpy Johnson!" Calvin manages to say.

"Who?"

Andre jumps out of bed and helps Calvin apply pressure, leaning in with his shoulder.

"Somebody is in the house!" Calvin says, "Grandpa caught me sneaking food, and… and he said there was a house slave that catches little slaves and breaks their bones and—"

Andre interrupts angrily, "Wait, what—Grandpa Wood said. Ugh, Calvin, stop!" He stops and grabs Calvin by his shoulders, pulling him away from the door. "Grandpa Wood was messin' with you, Calvin!" Andre flips on the light switch, awakening Kevin.

"Why the light? What's up?" Kevin signs before Andre signs back.

Andre signs back, "Don't worry, go back to sleep, Kevin."

Calvin continues in fear and frustration, "No, it's the truth! Grandpa Wood said! He is standing at the door, ready to break all my bones!"

Laughter comes from the opposite side of the door. "Ha! Ha! Ha! Ha! Ha! Ha!"

Andre swings open the bedroom door, revealing Grandma Odessa and Grandpa Wood, hardly containing their laughter. Each having one arm tucked in their matching pajamas and the other reaching into the room. They nearly fall to the floor laughing. Calvin immediately starts crying. Andre rolls his eyes and returns to his bed.

"Aww, my poor baby boy, Grandma is so sorry. Come here, baby," says Grandma Odessa. She composes herself and embraces Calvin with open arms.

"I bet your tail won't be eating all my damn leftover sweet potato fries no more, will ya?" Grandpa Wood says between bouts of laughter.

"Oh, stop, Wood. He gets it," Grandma Odessa says in a regretful tone. With a kiss to Calvin's forehead, she sends him to bed. "Now ya'll, get some sleep because we got the water park tomorrow!"

"Yay," the brothers say.

After the ruckus settles, and the lights are turned off, and everyone is in bed, Calvin stares at the ceiling. *What was that smell* that made him retch? Was it his mind playing tricks on him? Doubt floods over him like sweat on a Georgian summer.

"Get some sleep." Andre says, turning over.

"Okay," Calvin sniffles in response.

Calvin positions himself, his thoughts growing smaller and smaller as a comfortable position is found. A few burps and stomach gurgles later, he is fast asleep. And when he dreams, the dreams come like waves. He sees Stumpy Johnson many times, just as terrifying as the last, and just as many times as he is caught, Calvin kills him. Just as savage as the previous, every dream sequence starts the same way—a gun, a fork, a shoestring. Calvin would sneak down the stairs, the way he did earlier that night, opening the refrigerator and seeing a piece of food on a brass plate with a brass fork. The piece of food is indistinct but tantalizes Calvin's eyes. Impulse leads to a song sung that Calvin can't quite understand.

The dream cycle ends with the boy opening the refrigerator and waking up to the smell of Grandma Odessa's greasy, cheesy potatoes and bacon.

Calvin never awakes from his slumber to steal food the rest of the summer. And better yet, he never dreams of Stumpy Johnson after that night, and Stumpy Johnson was forgotten.

There is a drawn-out farewell from Calvin and his siblings by Grandma Odessa and Grandpa Wood. Many kisses and lingering hugs. Calvin embraces Grandpa Wood for the last time that summer. The last summer he would spend with all of his brothers at once.

Waves and kisses through the window of the train. And soon his grandparents are as small as ants. The boys settle in comfortably for the familiar, yet long, seven-hour train ride home to Figstern, North Dakota.

Calvin and his brothers adapt to life at home effortlessly, returning to routine as quickly as they left it. Since that night in the kitchen with Grandpa Wood, Calvin has no want or need to sneak food at night, not even to ask for seconds. In turn, Calvin loses weight, and the weight he loses brings on praise from his parents. Soon, school begins, and so does the discomfort and anxiety of sixth grade.

Calvin begins to have a recurring nightmare of eating in the cafeteria. Blurred faces cheer him on, and with every plate he licks clean and spoonful he swallows, cheers grow louder and louder. Raising his arms in victory as the last dish is finished, he is hoisted on the shoulders of the blurry-faced enthusiasts. A crown tilts on his head. A sash is gifted across his chest that reads *North Dakota's Greatest Eater*. The blurry-faced individuals throw him onto the floor. He appears so full he can't roll over on his belly. A giant fork descends from the clouds, and the crowd roars with laughter. The fork impales him, lifting him past the clouds to the giant fork holder sitting atop a refrigerator.

Calvin awakes from the nightmare with a grumble in his belly. Calvin tosses and turns; every growl and gurgle causes him to sit up with unease. He reaches for a cup of water on his bedside table, which sits there for when he wants to eat, but the cup is empty. He hates bathroom water, so he stands in his doorway devising a plan in which he would fetch water from the kitchen.

Calvin tiptoes past his older brother's bedroom. He's now out of practice in the act of food robbery and notices it is darker in the house than he remembered. So dark, he stubs his toe two or three times before reaching the kitchen.

With measured pace, Calvin fills his water glass. As soon as it is filled, he drinks until it is empty. Filling the cup again, he notices a vertical streak of golden light out of the corner of his eye. Turning his head, he sees a glow from the refrigerator. He places the water cup on the black-and-white marble countertop. Wanting to close the door, he can't help but pull it open after a rumbling grumble. To his chagrin, nothing looks appetizing to his talkative belly. Before he closes the door, he sees something wrapped in an icy covering of cellophane towards the back of the refrigerator.

Calvin reaches for the cellophane-covered mystery, unwrapping carefully. The plate wears a note, *Mom's treat! Do not touch!* There sat a hefty portion of blueberry pie—half frozen, half coagulated.

Calvin scoops a mouthful onto the plastic fork, careful not to spill it, and opens his mouth. Calvin eases the fork through his lips and closes his eyes with glee and pleasure. With every chew, Calvin thinks about the next fork and the next, and the next. The hair rises on the back of his neck as he hears:

"Greedy, greedy little Negro…" *Thump… slide.*

Calvin freezes as if in a trance, and tears fill his eyes. Goosebumps pour in bigger and bigger waves as his nose meets a familiar fusty odor of rot wafting through the night air.

"… Using the night for one's own plunder…." *Thump… slide.*

Calvin stands erect and turns his head towards the voice.

There stands a patchy silhouette of a one-armed man, bone thin; his clothing barely hanging onto his frail frame.

"Greedy, Greedy little Negro…" *Thump... slide.* The stride is solid and accurate without hindrance. "Let this club cure your hunger…" *Thump... slide.*

Its simper reveals its greasy-toned huddle of teeth. One milky white eye drifts, coming and going as it pleases. "Greedy, Greedy little Negro…" *Thump... slide.*

Calvin's left-hand shoots in front of him, searching for the nearest counter space. His feet glide atop the kitchen floor, slipping and sliding as he fights a pull with every bit of strength he can muster.

"Eating Massa out of house and home…" *Thump... slide.*

His left hand doesn't move and is glued to the marble kitchen island, but Calvin has full function of the rest of his body.

"No! Please no! Mommy! Dad! DAD! Please help!" Calvin screams at the top of his lungs.

Just then, the light down the opposite end of the hallway turns on, and Calvin looks in that direction. As he looks back, Stumpy Johnson is gone. But Calvin's hand remains on the counter. Try as he might, and indeed, he tries with furious tugs and pulls, he can't remove his hand. Though his hand is stuck, he feels relief. But soon the light from the hall blinks, then turns off. Calvin screams an unintelligible, wailing cry. Not before looking over his shoulder and seeing Stumpy Johnson raise a club high.

"Greedy, Greedy little Negro—"

With every thwack of the club, Calvin's body jounces and jumps in pain as his throat does not execute sound. His eyes water as he looks over to see the splash of his own blood meet Stumpy Johnson's decaying, dripping flesh. He sends an unmoving leer down at Calvin, a smile slathered upon his rotting face. Stumpy Johnson's cheeks quiver with every impact, shaking the island violently and cracking the granite.

REPATRIATE

POETRY COLLECTION

Jon Jon Stefan

Mall World

We are the only thing we have left to sell.
First hand—
I've seen you window shopping
through mirrors
photo albums.
I was window shopping through the back of a police car.
All features blurred under the $
now discounted $ hat you wear.

Still white mannequins
receding while this pig rants
about being oppressed
like he was the one in cuffs.
Like I had him hostage.
The line that ran through him,

a thrift store holding his life
second hand.

A new off-branding,
a new re-shelving
for the naked jungle of braille
with all the tongues of an economy.

And that's where I found bedrock
on the tongue of America
where there's nothing left but mall cops
one per capita.

There you will look like a duck,
swim like a duck,
and quack like a duck,
but squeal like a pig.

Gasleak Talking Points

And these people
who are so sick on their own saliva

they talk
and they kiss
and they spit
                just to spit.

They don't have to accept even what they want.

Gratefulness?
Modesty?

These whore-headed con men?

So, who will say thank you?
So, who will say excuse me?

Why would I admit ugly
in my violent beauty?

When will I beat a gas leak
in a chess tournament?
I will step on gravity
until it whimpers under me.

And I will be wonderful.
And I WILL live forever
on your hatred and worship.

I will protect us.
I will protect us.
I won't let another hair fall off your head.

Black Bile

Black bile spat out of the neck of your cigarettes.
Our melancholic humor flushed the rust down our postures.
We brought knives and lighters to the beach like an arms race.
We've probably killed each other so many times.
Just in case.
You'll see those best friends drooling ash onto the rocks, even now.
Fingers flower out of lint and thumbtacks.

Calloused

His brain used to be
like a ball of blisters
pink, bubbling, warm
most of all painful,
a stirring
under the hood of his skull.

Once he saw
an endless row of houses,
connected
like a nervous system
instead of the busy city,
where you could hear a gunshot
followed by bored silence.

Every prick in the ground buzzed
from house to house to house
and these houses were kingdoms.
a zone where you could say,
"this is mine."

In this,
you were right,
and always respected.
This was the end
of the American dream.

He wakes up.
His brain is now a shell of cracking calluses.
A row of clams

huddled around a cold, salty pearl.
He looks down the street
and snaps with every twig.
Like a junky without a fix.
He looks over his lawn
picking at a gun
that isn't there.

Panic Attack

As if she was guided by the tracers of a ghost,
She pulled herself forward
and ducked
under shoulders of linen, cotton, noisy fabrics.

She felt, not clearly,
but strongly,
feet stamping behind.
She heard,
not literally,
whirring voices.
Almost like instruments being tuned
before erupting in front of an audience.
She squeezed her temples between palms.
The crowd made a track for the chase.
They stared at her.
And they only stared at her,
with the fear and disgust she'd hope
for the assailant.
Yet, she couldn't look at herself.
She was hardly
a thing anymore.
When she screamed,
it ran over her thoughts

like white-out.

Now—
there was only a city street.

Then—
there was a woman on her knees.

and then—
a traffic jam resuming.

Repatriate

What shapes are these?" I asked.
"They're weed-shaped," he said about each of them.
"This is a weed shape."
"This is a weed shape."
Forming a calloused talon over them
"This is the other shape. They fit together perfectly."
Putting his hands on my flowers—
"Like yin to yang," he pulled one from the ground
and curling my fingers around another thorny flower,
I flinched away
and I cried so wastefully.

I hear a ? sound,
then form the shape
to pluck it from its source.
I see a ? heart
cupping my hands.
I scoop it. Homeward bound.
Braille to be wiped, jagged horizons

cradled in palm lines, our arrested future.
Have the windpipes always been this
ergonomical?

I hear this tic
fidgeted between your lips till your jaw hangs slack.
I see that rag.
America
dancing with pictures of snakes and red banners.

And there's the shape,
the other shape,
swooping over my shoulders now.
Kids who walk
and talk
like me
will be released
from the cracking pavement.

TOUGH MEAT

Quiana

The instructor asked, "when did you let fear stop you?"

I cringed at an emerging memory, wanting to remember a different time. Something less vexing, something safer to share if pressed. Nothing else came to mind. Just my sophomore year of high school. *That* memory, *that* fear, scratched to be unearthed, but even the recollection shortened my breath.

Weiland School of Arts, 1988. Trombones, clarinets, and cymbals played the melodies of Coltrane, Monk, and Miles. On the second floor, overlooking the football field, young pianists rehearsed on electronic keys. From the musical theater room, where I lived in a commune of thespians, four-part harmonies oozed. We studied the language of Rodgers and Hart, practicing harmonies with, and lyrics upon, one another. Singing, tapping, swaying, sachet-ing as we closed in on performances.

"5, 6, 7, 8—" Another dimension. Another existence.

At 5:45 a.m., bus 831 came. I waited on a corner where addicts wandered, where strawberries sold their bodies, where johns offered me rides that I knew not to take. I waited in the darkest dark until the beaming eyes of a yellow Falkor arrived, rescuing me from the inner-city blues. It transported me to the Oz of arts filled with music, dance, costumes, hopes.

I sang soprano in Mr. Lester's vocal ensemble with other campus misfits who dreamt in color. Those who didn't wear backpacks but carried sheet music and Variety magazines in their satchels. Boys who wore bowties and experimented with eyeliner. Girls who talked too much or too little with over-accessorized denim jackets. We bonded over quests for greatness and staged musicals that allowed us to don new personalities, different identities, other worlds.

"8, 7, 6, 5…"

"Davida wants to fight you," Ebony announces, unable to control her lips' curl. These girls were not bussed into the magnet program. They were the local students who congregated on the other side of campus where I took my general classes.

"I don't know Davida," I said.

I knew who she was, but I didn't really know her. No previous entanglement or conflict took place to warrant Ebony's announcement, but that didn't matter. I experienced enough violence from girls who simply chose not to like me. I pretended not to know why, because as soon as I admitted what I knew, I became what they believed and said.

"She stuck up."
"She think she so smart."

"She think she so cute."
"Who dat bitch think she is, anyway?"

If they only knew. *Dat bitch* didn't like herself any more than they liked themselves. *Dat bitch* was scared to death. *Dat bitch* spent enough time in their abusive audience, being pummeled by their collective fists. Fists to "f**k up her face."

Light-skinned girls who walked too tall received more than their share of negative attention. But I had to walk tall. I spent too many days sleeping on pallets and sheltering in basements of extended family. The perpetual new girl at school—always the new meat to devour—I had to, at least, be tough meat to chew.

Girls like me, like Davida, inherited violence as culture. We ate generations of trauma as morning grits. Verbal abuse, fermented from 17th century plantations, came mingled in our milk.

Those in power over us ruled by the whip, the fist, assault of the tongue, or the zip of a zipper. Authority figures beat the pride and freedom out of us, and some—like Davida—pursued the pride and freedom in others, just to be on the better side of the power dynamic.

Davida scheduled our brawl as a calendar event. I waited for her outside of the appointed bathroom. Because I had been jumped many times before, accepting such invitations left little room for unexpected beat-downs after school. As she approached, I wiped exhausted tears from my cheeks. She saw them and surprised me with pity. Instead of an ass-whooping, she hugged me. *Well, this is new*, I thought.

"Let's be friends," she said.
"Let's dress like twins," she said.
"Spend a night at my house," she said.
"Let's make love," she said.

Davida touched me like her daddy touched her. My body trembled in a peculiar way. The thrill felt like cold electricity shooting up my spine, more intense than allowing a boy's hands down my pants. But it didn't feel good. It felt like violence. Like intrusion. Inner-city girls like me often experienced intrusion long before nature spotted our underwear with blood.

I froze in a valley of decision. I didn't want her to hate me or beat me up. I only wanted a safe place to exist. A friendship to experience belonging, a home without pallets. So, with the same courage it took to take myself to the bathroom event, I removed her hand from my breast.

She turned over, pretending she wasn't angry.

"It's not you, it's me," I said.

"If I swung that way, I'd be flattered," I said.

But it wasn't long before Davida wanted to f**k up my face again. Her previous hate grew branches of rejection. She cursed my name and credibility, probably in fear I might curse hers first. But I never told her secrets, and yet she spilled my secrets like blood.

In the end, my sanctuary—the school where I finally found acceptance—morphed into halls that accused, lied, raged, and lurked with cruelty from Davida and circles who feared her. So, right before my senior year, I left Weiland School of Arts and enrolled in my local school. A music-free institution that derailed my dreams, where I never heard that invigorating count, "5,6, 7, 8…"

When did I let fear stop me?

The year before graduation. I allowed fear to prevent me from singing four-part harmonies in dimensions of acceptance. It disallowed me to be *extra* in a school where *extra* was the perfect way to be. And I can't resurrect the chance to walk across Weiland's stage for my diploma no more than I can resurrect a dead friend.

A million mistakes have been woven into the fabric of my character—most of which I don't regret. But if I could, I would undo the quitting of 1988. Fear was the real villain to overcome, and it abides in the same hallway as purpose. Now, I know to decline its invites, to ignore its accusations and threats. Fear can only be defeated with unapologetic boldness and a relentless stride. The truth is—fear can't stop anyone who refuses to be stopped.

LOVE

Section 4

ME AND MY HAIR

POETRY COLLECTION

Jana Ross

Protective Style

She is growing her hair like a blanket around her body.

Moss Woman
hangs her head in a river.
She has spent a lifetime learning about
herself,
and found that
she has to start by loving herself.
This often means an investment in bound-
aries.
After the current has cleansed her,
she casts a protection spell around her home,
but the one beside her bed each night is a body of
stone
and sinks into her room of dirt.

This lover who watches her
looks hungrily,
"Can you give me a thousand strands?
That is but a limb to a tree."
"No," she replies. "If I do, I shall bleed."
So, the lover looks at the ground and rips up vines and
leaves—
"I build my own."

But every handful of Earth,
each taking of life,
put a pain in her side
until she was curled around her crown.
And when the lover returned,
proud of the mimicry,
viewed not the limp body of the Moss Woman,
but instead, where she laid, a great Syca-
more.

Work Braids

She hauls long black braids over her shoulder
with the swing of her neck
like a crane raises its beak from rushing water.
This movement is done without thinking.
For weeks and months,
the braids watched her write and read,
and cry and bleed
and scrub and sweat
and laugh and fret.

Aunties

Shrieking women
are laughing
are loving
and leaning
on each other
are cleaning
and screaming
and heaving
and believing
in each other

with eyes closed
and hearts open
ages young
still bold
old too
still fun.

I love these women.

ILLNESS AND SLOW FOOD

Kay Lopez

I was fortunate not to have lost anyone during the Covid crisis. We were all holding our breaths, hoping the respiratory infection that would swiftly take the lives of almost seven million worldwide might spare us and our most beloved. I read Christina Sharpe's *In the Wake: On Blackness and Being*, which contextualises being "in the wake" as a continuous present, one that situates the afterlives of slavery as flow—ongoing, overlapping. According to Sharp, being "in the wake," is how we attend to questions of care and the structural lack of care for Black life of which the Covid disaster exposed. Being "in the wake" is also an aftermath, echoing much of my grief work. I thought back to some of the pandemic's quietest moments, in which I, like many, sought anchorage from its tumultuous uncertainty.

To my surprise, although it's proved useful now, literature would not become my port of refuge. When lockdown arrived in England, we had hardly anywhere to go, except for indoors—both inside of the house and inside of ourselves. Text messages received from close friends and family resonated with the idea that everything was all-consuming—there were no next steps. Any previous plans were now on indefinite pause. This moment of collective quiet, although freeing in parts, became one of excavation which opened me up and hollowed me out. There I was, looking out towards the street from my third-floor Lewisham flat. As I began to reflect, it dawned on me that I, like many city-dwellers, were no longer a part of the rat-racers, hustling to get the train on time, or cyclists weaving in and out of traffic—helmetless and hurried. And none of this was likely to happen again for a long time. As Zadie Smith writes in her essay collection *Intimations*, we were all scurrying around with no-where to go, looking for "something to do." So, with this in mind of which I struggle to recall a direct symptom of hunger, I thought, maybe I'll cook.

Before the pandemic, by a mixture of cultivation and chance, I was offered an opportunity to have a restaurant in South-East London. I am not one to keep a detailed log of the things I have completed, which upon reflection isn't so much about fulfilment's absence, but rather the reality that such accomplishments have been out of absolute necessity. Yet, this particular success happened in a serendipitous manner, and there was little evidence it would work. But the owner took a risk, and my partner and I (at the time) accepted. In retrospect, we had little idea what would eventually become of this, but we agreed. On the restaurant's debut, we miraculously sold out.

In the weeks leading up to the opening, we brainstormed what we might cook. For me, it was obvious, and my partners graciously agreed. We'll make stew. It was a vegan restaurant, and I began conjuring my grandma's meatless recipes. I considered oxtail stew, but without the ox or the tail. As we brainstormed vegan menu alternatives, it became obvious to make gluten from scratch. Yes—the protein strain naturally found in certain grains.

Gluten gives dough its elasticity, binding it together, giving it the stretchy quality we're familiar with. The process is one that my grandmother taught her three daughters and grandchildren. Make a ball of dough—a 3:1 ratio of flour to water. When the ball is formed, begin to wash it under water, and you do, separate the starch compound from the glutinous protein compound. It's a long, tenuous process of three, four, or sometimes five washes, but the results are beautiful and transformative. The murky, starchy water washes down the sink (similar to washing rice), and you're left with a firm, elastic, beige blob—gluten.

As a child, I was fascinated by the process and still am. It's a long and laboured undertaking, working through the grief food and the grief work; stretched thin, expanded, collapsed. Gluten makes up only about 15-20% of wheat's property. Starch, the other 75%. So, as you might imagine, after spending an hour working and washing the flour, it diminished to half its size.

I'd not made gluten alone before—not without my supervising grandmother. Yet even in her absence, the beauty of her legacy and tradition prevailed. There I was, working at a small coffee shop in South-East London, miles and miles away from my Toronto home, even farther away from my grandmother's home in Manchester parish, Jamaica. I was given the opportunity to revitalise our history in her memory. In the pandemic's quietest moments, a desire emerged to overlap a part of the past onto the present. For in the first months of the crisis, we listened eagerly and anxiously for what was to follow. Two hours of the daily news looping the number of virus outbreaks within 100 metres of your home; how the government's economic priorities failed the medical system, how the country's money was running out, and peoples' patience, running thin. And yet, in the eye of the storm was the rare possibility for moments of soothing quiet.

I was reluctant to write about food with the risk of redundancy. Throughout much of the pandemic, many were cooking, and the rest were writing about it. Food stories pervaded the internet—of banana breads, sourdough false-starts, and kombucha scobys that exploded in the cupboard. But a slightly more complicated narrative simmered beneath the obvious. We were in a state of collective grief. I realised that I had been grieving for a long time. Grieving the physical distance between me and my family, grieving relationships that changed, some of which needed to and others I still painfully longed for. I was in grief, for things I'd forgotten to write down, and language that had escaped me. I was grieving myself while grappling with my departure from religion and its residual losses, particularly of community. So, I made gluten and with it, I made stew.

On most Sundays of my earlier childhood, we'd make stew of all kinds, always without meat, and usually with Jamaican seasonings. It was a thing, after spending busy Saturdays in church, to spend Sundays at home.

Sundays were slow days. My father played vinyl records, often classical music, and pottered around the garden. My mother attended laundry and aided me in getting my things sorted for the week ahead. None of this was rushed, nor was our Sunday meal, which my father, the more devoted cook, began in the early part of the afternoon. I can't recall our dinnertime—it's a blur in my mind, but six o'clock is a reasonable assumption as we were similar to most. The thing I think my father, and many others, enjoy about cooking stew is that it can be left alone. You can put the lid on and walk away, do other things, and return to it in due course. It's less consequential than, say, a steak. The pressure for accuracy is less impending, and there is more room for repair in the event of error. It's forgiving. There's temporal flexibility—room to attend to other things in the meantime.

The urge to make stew became a way of doing Sundays, of redoing Sundays. A comfort amid the unravelling world around us. I wanted to bring something back to life. In the rhythm of stew, there is a likening to grief. In the beginning, when you first receive the saddening news that a loved one has died, it's a shock to the pan. It's like making brown stew chicken of Jamaican cuisine. One coats the chicken in brown sugar and spices whilst waiting for the searing oil to arrive at the required temperature. Once it's "to temp," you place the raw chicken, now exposed to the environment, into the bubbling oil and brown it in a shroud of caramelisation. The rest of the process is a relationship of which you have mild participation. It's largely unprovoked—high heat to seal the meat, low heat to simmer, reduce, waiting for the stew to come to a finish.

My father phoned me to tell me he had been diagnosed with Parkinson's disease. A series of tests ruled out essential tremors, a neurological disorder causing hands, head, and voice to tremble. But we knew something was wrong. Tremors are mostly manageable, but this is not true of Parkinson's disease. In the fourth year of my father's diagnosis, his aggressive condition began to intrude upon his day-to-day activities. He processed the diagnosis, and its interference, with religious consolation. Since I departed from religion ten years ago, that framework no longer sufficed for me. Instead, the metaphor of slow food offered something larger than language.

The metaphor, of peripheral interest, was how I continued to work through the collective grief of the global disaster and the reality of my father's illness. And while many were on apps, learning to speak a second language, my father's body forgot its first. A man of profound stature was now living with a disease that resounded as a shock to the pan. This disease, like oil, would clog his ability to taste, smell, and move over time. On some days the symptoms were as though the kitchen power shut off. On others, my father is lidded and comfortable. On the worst days, illness is like a pot boiling over, and you rush to turn off the stove, in an urgent attempt to cool the invasive symptoms and arrest its molecular system. Here I was, leaning over the sink in my South-East London flat, untangling the gluten from the wheat, taking time I had been given to work through the dough, and subsequently, the grief.

In Caribbean heritage, slow food is a prominent part of the culinary tapestry. There are recipes central to the culture like the pepper pot, a food with First Nations origins by "people who were there hundreds and hundreds of years before the colonies." In the *Eccles Centres' Caribbean*

Foodways Oral History Project, Guyanese cook Hazel Daniels speaks of the creolisation of Caribbean food. The adaptability permeates its culinary tradition, namely the pepper pot. Its key ingredient is cassareep, made from boiling cassava for hours until the root's flesh becomes dark. According to Daniels, the "magical preservation quality of the cassareep means that this rich stew, which is made from combining meat, fish, or vegetables with the dark sauce, both receive change and convey survival which signal the Caribbean's central historical theme: cultural endurance." This was the comfort of Sunday stew, the continuity of memory, of cultural tradition, of more time, and slow food.

Slow food forgives more than its counterpart if you get the first few stages right. Of the rest, you're likely to succeed. Throw this and that into the pot, cover it, and you're mostly free to take care of other things. Stew doesn't boil over, like pasta. It doesn't burn quickly, like a fillet of fish. Unlike baking, it's a little less precise; you have room in the event of error, and time to correct it. If you add too much salt, you can usually add water to rectify it. If you add too little salt, you simply put more in. Sunday's slow time, stew, and slow foods are functions of longevity and intricate parts of tradition. Some things were gone, I knew—but not all had been lost.

On one of the many days of the crisis that seemed to blur into one another, my father phoned to say although he was now a revisiting vegetarian, he purchased take-away oxtail stew. I smiled. And maybe he heard my lips pull away from my teeth, because he then laughed with guilty pleasure. Illness changes the body, without permission and without warning. The symptoms of Parkinson's disease meant my father could no longer smell or taste. But he said he could feel "its heat" on his face. There—he imagined the past. For him, it wasn't about what was any longer, or what was lost along the way. It was about being still, being slow—in the meantime—in the wake.

THE LONELINESS OF SHADOWS

POETRY COLLECTION

Veripuami Nandee Kangumine

The day you found out
you weren't really dying,
a moth lands on your arm
and unfurls its wings
while you sit in your doctor's
waiting room.

The walls claim he attended
The University of Cairo.
Egyptian memorabilia sits
on the shelf next to the breast cancer
awareness poster,
like he misses the Nile—
like he misses home.

After lunch he sits you down
on the bed in the corner behind
a thin curtain
and presses his latex forefingers
into your abdomen,
feeling for any signs of tenderness
or grief.

Takes note of your breathing,
pinches your skin,
watches it retract,
looks at your gums,
your tongue,
notes your dehydration
and delusions.

His office smells like a tomb.
The lighting doesn't help much, either.
The picture of the pyramid of Giza
hangs on a single pin
next to the poster of fibroids
like a warning.

His face looks a lot like a lost tooth.
When he helps you up
his hands are brittle—
like he has had to start over
too many times.

As you wait for him to diagnose you,
you want to tell him,
he is the sixth doctor you have seen,

and no one can seem to find
anything wrong with you.
You want to ask him to prescribe something
for the homesickness
that you feel in your bones,
but you don't want to tell him
how to do his job.

The White Linen Swaying in the Wind

After I offer to wash her clothes
in the washing machine,
Ma refuses—
angry at how easy we have it—
says she will do it herself
in the old cast iron tub,
like they used to do back in the olden days.

When I ask if I should carry laundry outside,
she stares at her hands for a long time
(I think she forgets about my offer),
but then she begins the story
of the year she worked on a farm.

She never mentions who owned the farm
in any of her stories.
It is as if the person's color
is removed completely—
a shadow in black and white photograph.

When she talks about the work she did on the farm,
or the years she spent on the outer banks of the river,
collecting tobacco leaves to dry sell to the big store owners,
she never mentions their color either.

But we all knew no one with our color
owned a farm or a store
or even their own hands
not in those days anyways.

Then she goes quiet again—
remembering how the fibers of her fingers
would hurt after scrubbing in between
the cracks of farm houses

or how her back would hurt
washing up after other people's children.
She could not even touch her own children
or even give them a bath.
She eventually had to send them away,
to live with a distant aunt.
No one asked who their father was.

When I ask what she meant by touch,
she would look at her hands
opening and closing them
as if they weren't hers but a stranger's.

Finally, she told me
after spending the bad part
of a cold July morning
wringing out the old linen to dry

by the hanging line
that her hands froze in that shape.

Later at home while washing the little ones,
she found herself with her hands
around her last born,
trying to get the blood to come out—

wringing so hard.
Later, when she was asked,
she said, she thought
he was a linen sheet.

Red Sand

At the Hosea Kutako International Airport
my sister kisses the tarmac
before she gets on the plane
and leaves for work in the UK.

She gets on all fours
and presses her lips to the ground.
For a mere second
it looks like she is praying—

or looks like the time
after buying bread from the corner store,
we saw a woman kneeling on the ground,
eating sand and spitting the grains out.

Veripuami Nandee Kangumine

Sometimes the iron in the blood
is not enough for two, my sister explained
after pointing to the woman's protruding stomach.

She calls after three months,
says she was settling in
finding a place to stay and work,
and a mobile carrier for long distance calls,

says it's not easy
and the weather isn't forgiving like back home,
says she can sometimes go weeks
without seeing the sun.

When she calls after six months,
she sounds different
like a stranger.
She says she got a permanent job in a hospice.

Says she'll send for me
when she is really settled in
I wonder if that means
when she finally sounds like the locals.

On other days when she calls
she says the homesickness is so strong.
That bakery below the room
she shares with three other women

smells like butter churning
in the calabash.
She says it smells exactly like the butter
Auntie Tukoo used to churn using only her feet,

says if she finds someone coming home
she will send her old clothes
and that I should send
a little bit of the red sand

from underneath of my left shoe
back with them to the UK
so she always knows where I am.

After she stops calling
I count the days,
then I stop counting
and I stop waiting.

CAUTIOUS INCARCERATION

POETRY COLLECTION

Margaret Ajakaiye

Her life floats by—
no ripple nor stir—
a standstill in the depth of time.

The waters are heavy,
almost hot,
calcified by old laughter and stubborn memories
inside a brown bird paces, gently—
clubbed feet and a battered eye.
But she still wonders
whether the sun will come?
Or if her wings will shake off their gloomy robes
and the water befriend sweetness again?

This pond, like many others is empty—
not a reflection to be found.
The wings that once flapped and eyes that once saw, wounded.
So, she waits for the sun
in cautious incarceration.

Shape Shifter

Is she part of my story?
The unwelcome pervasive lodger
"I'm sure you changed your locks, *twice*"
or perhaps she's the narrator,
the cursive penpal, eager to interrupt at any moment
with lashes of ink and a plethora of painful storylines

Is she in the audience?
Quiet and watching, critical of the plain and simple
itching for a jump scare
or conceivably the main character,
performing her dramatic dues and awaiting applause.
Sorrows and indeed many prayers erupt from the crowd, eventually.

Is she a contractive stomachache?
Commanding throbs of cliffhangers and pangs of hindsight
or perhaps the bubbling reflux once all seems well and gone

like a bad breath on a stormy day
or thick sweat in June heat.
Whatever she is, she lingers on
shifting in all *her* ways.

Text Messages

Do you wanna exchange vocal vibrations?" she types sheepishly.
She catches herself
in the reflection of a silent screen,
the usual furrowed thick brows,
needle eyes and chapped lips.
Her glossy fingers stationed on the keyboard, at the ready.

She blames the connection
or perhaps the screen is stubborn—
an inch shy from desperation.

"Fine" she hisses.

Scratches emerge on her Poundland screen protector.
"I'll share my vibrations and citations with someone else
cuz my ululations don't match the rhythm of your soul.
The only time we meet is when our sound waves crash
and amount to nothing."

Empty.

"Endless typing ain't nothing but you piping smoke dreams—
cloudy hurrahs, but who gets the last laugh?"

She was anticipating that precipitation,
waiting for the rain to hit
and quench her thirst—the social loneliness.

But it didn't come.
Ever.

Train 48

When a deep breath isn't deep enough,
and even the sea refuses to swallow,
I look to you.

To fly beyond a bird,
and suckle beyond a child,
to believe beyond a saint,
that rest and restoration
still exists, even now.

Bucket List

I wrote a bucket list
for you.
Scribbles in a foreign language
on the third shelf.
I collected them all,
with a bucket and yellow spade.
Scoops of your timely highlights,
prescription joy from a package deal.
We'll unravel under the searing sun,
crimson like the sorbet,
sipping on your delirious laughter,
with screeching tan lines on pigment skin.
I penned it for the moment you stop glowing,
and we know that your time is fading away.
We'll pick one,
one by one, until we reach that day—
when the light dims behind your eyes
and you need no longer stay.

BLACK LOVE UNSPOKEN

Elizabeth Best

Before Emancipation, it was unsafe for Black folks to show
love for children and spouses, who could randomly be taken.
So love was felt, reined in, variously inferred but hardly spoken.
Black wisdom warned that coddled hearts would be easily broken.

After Emancipation, it was not necessary to speak Black love
in a one-room house that squatted on stacks of stones –
packed like spaced-out teeth in an ear-to-ear smile –
that let wild ducks slip through to lay and stray dogs to die.
Black love sprawled across the linoleum-covered room
and made space for three pairs of legs that had raced
down Jacob's Ladder and across Condemn Gully
to tire themselves skipping Double Dutch, running relays
or scrambling up fenced-in trees to snatch forbidden fruit.
Black love circled torn toenails, swabbed knees bruised skinless,
filled three extra bowls of victuals from servings meant for four,
expanded into morsels scraped together to feed one more.

After Emancipation, it was not customary to preach Black love
when a grandmother's warm kisses cooled knuckles
grown to twice their size from playing marbles for "knucks"
with boys who packed spite into each taw crashed into my paws.
Black love dripped into the barely bearable Epsom salts bath
and hot castor oil massage that scattered bruised blood
from joints with the same invasion of pain as the original hit.
All the while, Black love seeped out from her heart into muttered
one-line sermons that filled the space between each whimper
with warnings about cockroaches who learned too late why
they had been told not to accept invitations to roosters' dances
and glass bottles that stuck their necks into boulders' business.

After Emancipation, it was not necessary to broadcast Black love
when news of the church fair held no hope of new clothes
and a sister's long, old-fashioned, flared frock
packed away two years ago took on a close-fitting
newness to accentuate my recent teenage curves.
Black love rested in her promise that no one would recall the dress
since I filled it out as completely as a banana fitted its peel.
Black love lingered in her crimson nails that tapped my shoulders.
It later jingled in the triple-string necklace of red jumbie beads
she had threaded in secret to match the red polka dots
and the thin red belt that made my new/old dress look smart
and half-plugged the hole of want widening in my heart.

After Emancipation, it was not necessary to explain Black love
when I woke late, and the water barrel yawned to be filled
from the public pipe at Village End, a quarter mile away,
and a stepmother hated for me to grow up *spoilt* and lazy,
so I had to balance one pail on my head, one in each hand,
and turn a twenty-minute saunter into a ten-minute trot.
Black love always waited with the principal's thick leather strap
to sear the value of punctuality into my palm or back.
After school, Black love fed my appetite with man-sized dinners
but made me scrub pots and dishes to practice responsibility.
Before playtime, Black love held the ruler, ready to crack down
on digits that didn't carry one to the tens or hundreds column.

After Emancipation, it was not necessary to whisper Black love
when Dad placed half of his pay packet in Mama's purse,
gambled away the rest, borrowed back some and expected her to
conjure up breakfast and dinner all week, as well as fried pork,
dried peas and rice and baked macaroni and cheese on Sunday.
Black love often lured Dad's calloused palm to trace the upsweep
of Mama's French twist before bombarding her dimpled cheeks
and ruby pout with a never-ending barrage of smacking kisses.
Black love filled Friday night with throaty laughter, swayed under
rum and Coke and knew that Mama would save the last dance
for Dad, ignoring the leaner, more graceful movers, the better dressed,
and taxi home with his snoring head, heavy upon her breast.

So long after Emancipation, it is necessary to voice Black love
especially after reasoning, scolding, and shaming have not reined in
teenage hormones that bucked against reminders of parents' failures,
generational traumas and fears that stretched like speed bumps
across the path of every new venture and independent choice.
Black love must no longer hide beneath tough tongue-lashings,
expect the beloved's heart to espy its kind force and caring intent.
Black love must be aware that even adults need their egos soothed
or they will feel their self-worth being dragged below the baseline.
Black love must remember that children hungry for hugs and thirsty
for a spirit-lifting boost need to fully know, through tell and show,
the unequivocal love which young souls need to grow and glow.

So long after Emancipation, our people are slow to lavish love
on each other but are quick to spew caustic remarks as though
we see us as unlovable with the eyes of bigots and do not know
that self-hating reaps the contempt that we have learned to sow.

KINDA GREEN, KINDA BLUE

Monique Franz

I knew little about the war overseas. Just that it was all everybody talked about. And that more jobs opened up.

I cleaned for Mrs. Daniels, whose husband flew for the Air Force. She stood big and pregnant with her second child when she gave me a dress that changed my life.

"I can't fit this itty-bitty thing no more, Bessie," Missus said. "Take it." She threw it at me like a dishrag.

"Thank you, Ma'am," I replied, touching the cloth between my fingers. Flowers, the shade of an ocean, covered it from the neck to the hem.

"Pretty," I said. "What color is this?"

"It's teal," she replied. "Kinda green. Kinda blue."

Teal. Something about the color made me want to lie down in green pastures. I put the cloth up to my nose as though I could smell its blossoms. I couldn't wait to wear it to church and sit upright by those fancy girls who giggled at the wool dress I wore year-round.

The dress covered the bosom and flowed to the ankles, so it wouldn't warrant a licking from Daddy. A small tear hid under the armpit, but I figured as long as I kept my arms down, the dress would wear as good as new.

When I put it on that next Sunday, Mama twirled me around, hooting like a choo-choo train. Daddy sat over in his chair frowning, eyeing me from head to toe.

"Don't go acting like you somebody better than us with those white-folk clothes on," he said.

The words smacked the smile from my face. I wished he hadn't said what he said, but knowing Daddy, he was only mad the dress gave him no reason to call me a whore.

A week later, Daddy came home with news.

"Bessie, you know that boy Marcus from the church?"

"I think so," I lied. Marcus sat in the second row of the church, where he often smiled at me, and I'd smile back. That's all we did though.

Whenever a boy talked to a girl at church, all of Decatur, Alabama started wagging their tongues. Once I got whipped because a boy tried to shake my hand after service. Daddy accused me of "acting loose," so I never talked to anybody after that.

"Ain't Marcus one of the junior deacons who move chairs and stuff for the pastor?" I asked, pretending my memory was fuzzy.

"That's him," Daddy said. "You and him gonna get married."

"Huh?" I asked too sharply.

Daddy snapped his wild eyes at me, the same eyes he got before he smacked me across something.

I quickly fixed it. "I mean—yes, sir. But Daddy, how come that deacon boy doesn't want to court me first?"

"Courting leads to babies," Daddy said in a cutting tone. "If you don't believe me, ask your mama."

Mama's embarrassed eyes peeked up from the stove, then fell right back down into the pot she stirred.

"Don't worry about it," Daddy continued. "You going to marry that boy before you get into trouble. That's all."

Plenty of girls were getting into trouble, so I understood Daddy's meaning. I later learned from Marcus that he initially asked for permission to court me.

"Hell nah," Daddy told him. "You'd be courting, while she'd be the one left in the family way."

Marcus replied, "Sir, I have no ill intentions. I'm God-fearing."

"Is that right?" Daddy scoffed. "You either thinking marriage or you got ill intentions. Which one?"

"I'd be happy to marry your Bessie if you let me," Marcus said. "She's a nice girl who minds her pa, and everybody knows that."

"No way," Daddy said. "You got nothing to give her, and I need her around the house to help her mama and little brothers."

As quick as lightning, Marcus asked, "Don't you got a farm, sir?"

Daddy cut him an eye. "What you getting at?"

"If I be family, then you got yourself an extra hand, not one less."

That's all it took to turn Daddy around. He and Marcus made a deal, and I knew not to question Daddy more than I had. What he said went, and it went better for me to mind him. But the idea of marrying Marcus didn't bother me. He had friendly eyes, a medium build, hair cut neat and tight. His teeth were jagged though, like each one of them tried to escape his mouth in different directions. But his dimples fell so deep, you forgave his teeth.

Marcus was number five of eight children in the Jackson family. They lived a mile south in a shotgun shack no bigger than ours. His daddy drank the sense out of his head, so their oldest brother James reared Marcus and the rest of them. The other brother fancied juke joints like his father, but Marcus, like James, sought the straight and narrow.

The night before the wedding, Daddy arranged for Marcus to come over for dinner. I had to cook by myself that night. Mama polished the wood floors and wiped the soot from the walls. Daddy busied himself, hammering nails into the beam holding our tin roof.

"We're going to hang some sheets to make y'all a room for the time being," Daddy announced between the pounding. "In no time, me and that boy gon' build the add-on to the back of the house for y'all to keep private."

As Daddy hammered, I eyed the scars on his back. They were put there by some white folks who trained horses in town. They didn't like Daddy driving around their parts, and because a Negro has less value than a dog, there ain't no more good skin on Daddy's back. I figured that's why Daddy was mean. Not because of their whips, but because of his worth.

Marcus and I married in September as the weather cooled. Our folks paraded us around like horses that day. Daddy walked around with his chest puffed out like the town mayor, and Mama fussed over my hair every time she came near. All the while, me and Marcus grinned at one another, bashful-like, holding each other's sweaty hands.

Reverend Horace brought the whole church to watch us jump the broom. As soon as our feet hit the ground, the choir rose to sing "Down by the Riverside." Our families lost all restraint while celebrating. They clapped, and danced, and shouted, "Study war no more."

Daddy trotted over, his eyes watery and proud. He hugged and kissed me for the first time I could remember.

"Make sure you always have that boy's plate fixed and his bed warm, ya hear?"

I heard Daddy loud and clear. For the first month after the wedding, only a flimsy sheet stood between the newlywed mattress and my two brothers. But I kept the bed warm, even when Marcus was nervous. It wasn't long before we got the hang of each other, though.

My young husband eased into the family work as though he had always been a spoke in our wheel. He helped Daddy and my brothers reap the cabbage and sweet potato harvest, but had no shame peeling the yams with me and Mama in the kitchen. Meanwhile, Daddy whipped and fussed at the boys much less, and he stopped hitting me altogether.

"You's grown now," Daddy said. "You got to mind your husband—even before me."

Marcus never put his hands on me though, except to be fresh. On our walks to the woods, he'd tickle my sides, laboring for my laughter. Down by the creek, he and I kissed and did private stuff we didn't dare do with my brothers in the same room. In the woods, we were free to call out, to cry each other's names while the trees echoed back.

One day under the fall foliage, Marcus told me, "I'm gonna join the Navy."

I took in a long breath and said nothing. The smell of firewood drifted from a nearby farm, taking the bitter off the chill. Meanwhile, gold leaves trickled down from the upper branches, falling like tears.

"After I do my time in the Navy, we gon' move up north where colored folks make decent money," he said.

"What you want to move for?" I asked him.

"I can't take care no family moving rocks from one place to another for two dollars a day," Marcus said, "especially when I have to help your daddy work the farm too. So, I've been making plans—"

I chortled, not meaning to.

"What?" he asked, amused.

"Lord knows you gon' wear me out with all your plans."

"I had it in my plans to marry *you*… a long time ago," Marcus said, tapping my nose.

"Is that right?" I asked.

"Yup. And when I saw you in that pretty dress, I got the courage to ask your daddy about courting you."

"That was brave of you."

"It sure was. Those fellows at church were talking about how fine you was, but they were all scared to cross your daddy."

"And you weren't?"

"Heck yeah, I was. But I had to speak up. I wasn't taking no chances with the competition." Marcus traced the curves of my forehead, down the slope of my nose with his finger before pecking my lips. "What's on your mind, girl?"

"Nothing."

"Gotta be something," he said.

But I didn't know what to tell him. Nobody ever asked what I was thinking before he did. Whenever he asked this, I usually said the same old thing.

"Nothing."

"I know there's some good thoughts in that pretty head of yours. You lock them away like treasures."

"Mama told me women shouldn't say too much, especially around their men."

Marcus sucked his teeth. "If God didn't mean for women to talk, he'd give them beaks to coo like birds."

I laughed, trying to think of something meaningful to say. "There's something so beautiful and so sad about the leaves falling."

"Oh, yeah?" Marcus feigned interest.

"Yeah. They're kinda like memories. And we, like the branches, trying to hold on to them as long as we can."

"I'm gonna hold on to you as long as I can," Marcus said, grabbing onto one of my breasts.

I pushed his hand off. "How you gon' hold on to me? Going off to some navy at a time like this?"

"I'm trying to make a better life for you—for us," Marcus said. His face grew serious. "I can't stay in your daddy's house forever."

My mouth twisted at him. "I ain't asking you to."

"Sound like you is."

"Don't you go putting words in my mouth," I told him.

"Why you sass me, girl? I don't sass you."

I clamped my lips shut, bracing for a smack on the mouth. I thought for sure he might turn colors on me. Daddy turned colors all the time, going from smiling to beating in a manner of seconds. There were times I didn't know the last thing I did to set Daddy off before I picked myself up off the floor.

Marcus moved in slowly and kissed my lips again. "I was right about that pretty little mind of yours. You got lots to say, don't you?"

I laughed nervously, unsure if I was in the clear. "Pardon me. I got beside myself," I said.

"Not necessary." Marcus said, tracing my nose again. "It's better to hear your sass than worry about your silence."

I didn't know why I found it so easy to fuss with Marcus. The truth was, he didn't really scare me. I spent a lifetime scared of making folks mad, making them lash out. But no matter what I said to Marcus, he found a way to be kind.

We returned to the farm where my brothers played stickball in the field. Marcus ran over to them. "Who's winning? I wanna play."

"Play with us," they both chimed. My little brothers circled Marcus, grinning like it was dinnertime. I could tell by their faces that Marcus fed their souls like he fed mine.

I called after them, "Ya'll want some sweet tea? I can bring some from the house."

They sang in unison, "Yeah!"

Marcus put his arms around them both and pointed at me. "Looka here, fellas. See that girl right there, smiling?"

My brothers squinted in my direction, scratching their heads.

"When she looks good, I look good. I make it my business to make her smile and not cry, ya hear?"

The boys nodded, then glanced towards my daddy far off in the fields. They returned their attention back to the stick and the ball, but I'm sure they knew Marcus's meaning.

Anytime Daddy started fussing in the house, Marcus just walked out. He said his father was the same way, "a mosquito-itch from back-slapping somebody."

After Marcus had been with us a bit, my daddy knocked Mama off a chair. Marcus jumped to his feet so fast it startled everybody. Daddy jerked towards him as if to say, *Boy, I'd kill you if you try something.*

But Marcus wouldn't cross my daddy in his own house. He sat right back down, saying instead, "Sir, Mama Gladys gon' be good from now on."

Daddy looked down at Mama, whose eyes raced back and forth between them. Daddy looked around, embarrassed, before shooing Mama from his feet.

"Go on somewhere," he said.

Mama scurried away, out of sight.

Later that night, Daddy and Marcus chatted on the porch. Daddy started preaching about men being lord in their homes.

"The Bible say—'Wives, submit yourselves to your husbands as unto the Lord,'" Daddy said. "Husbands are the heads of their wives as Christ is to the Church."

Marcus quoted as fast as a backhand, "Yes, sir. The Bible also say—husbands ought to love their wives as their own bodies."

It grew silent—all but the toad croaks from the nearby river.

Daddy asked soberly, "What if you don't love yourself?"

The air got quiet before Marcus spoke again. "Sir, when there's war within, we make war without. When we fix our minds on peace, peace comes and the warring stops."

From that day, Daddy didn't hit Mama no more. He kept fussing and cussing, but I never saw my mama scurry from his feet again.

By the spring, Marcus set out to fulfill his plans to serve overseas. He predicted Daddy would put up a fight about the Navy, so he assured Daddy that he would send money back to the farm. Daddy liked that idea. So, Marcus marched down to the Huntsville recruiting office and enlisted for the sea.

The night before Marcus headed off to the Pacific, a million stars peppered the sky. I waited on the porch for him, counting the fireflies, while my kin went down to Aunt Bella's, so he and I could eat alone.

I put on his favorite dress with the teal flowers and pressed my hair with the hot comb. Dinner waited on the potbelly stove. Sour milk biscuits, yams, fried okra, and a steak I could never afford on my own.

I went to the butcher, having only thirty cents in my pocket, expecting to buy throwaway cuts of pork.

"Marcus is leaving to fight the Japanese," I told him. "So, I want to buy something for a stew."

"Don't you fuss about nothing," Mr. Leo said. "That Marcus is a good one. I'm gon' fix you up a good cut to send that boy off special."

And that he did. I nearly fell on the floor when I unwrapped a thin T-Bone steak when I got home. Boy, I watched that meat on the grill like it was a newborn baby.

Later that evening, Marcus appeared on the gravel road, wearing his navy whites. He walked straighter in his uniform. My smile grew as he got closer until he greeted me with a kiss. His eyes glistened with pride and sadness, the way Daddy looked when he and I jumped the broom.

I set dinner before Marcus that night and sat across the table. His eyes lit up when he saw the steak, but he hovered for a while, not saying a thing.

"What's wrong?" I asked. "Steak okay?"

"Oh yeah," he said.

"Then, what's wrong?"

"You know—colored boys fighting in the Pacific don't come back all the time?"

"You is," I told him, looking dead in his eyes. I shoveled yam into my mouth, smiling lest he thought I sassed him. "You gon' eat that steak or what?"

Marcus smiled and sawed the tender flesh with his knife. He threw a bite into his mouth, and his eyes rolled back the way they do when he's on top of me.

"Girl, I ain't never tasted nothing so fine in my life."

Marcus and I laughed, ate, talked, then we laid down in the back shed that he and daddy built. As we talked and giggled, he traced his finger from the bridge of my nose over my lips before kissing them. We'd talk some more, then again, he'd trace his finger from the bridge of my nose, over my lips and kiss me.

"Why do you do that?" I asked him.

"Beauty like yours ain't enough to just see with your eyes," he said. "I want to touch it, feel it with my fingertips."

My shoulders drew in, and my eyes fell low. "Why do you love me like you do?"

"How can I not?" he said. "It's the only thing I'm meant to do."

I still didn't understand, but I believed him. And we made love slowly, then held onto one another naked.

"I wish I could stop the world from spinning, have more time just like this," Marcus said. "But I want to make a better life for you."

"You've made my life so much better already," I told him.

The next morning, Marcus and I got up before dawn, trying not to wake my people, but Mama had already risen to warm porridge for breakfast. Daddy got the boys up and marched them around, issuing orders. The morning air felt thick, and we all moved somber slow.

Marcus donned the jacket of his uniform like his arms were heavy. He put his drawers, razor, and Bible in his duffle bag as though each weighed a ton. Then, he shuffled into the kitchen and flumped into a chair.

"Coffee?" I asked, handing him the tin cup.

Marcus grabbed my hand and held it tight for a long time. "I'm taking your flower dress with me," he said, grinning.

"What for?" I asked.

"So, I can smell it," he replied, winking. "And so you won't be wearing it for nobody else while I's gone."

We laughed, and the air got thinner. I sat across from him as he sipped, and we stared at each other, holding hands, wasting no energy on words. Our eyes said everything needed to be said, and everything we dared not say.

When the time had come, my family hugged Marcus goodbye on the porch. Afterwards, they went inside, and Marcus and I hugged as though trying to melt together.

"Be good now," Marcus said.

"Be safe," I replied.

We kissed one last time. Then, I watched him march off with that duffle bag, getting smaller and smaller on the stony path until he disappeared from sight.

I never saw him again.

Several of his letters came from overseas before I received that telegram from some men in uniform. I didn't cry at all. It didn't seem real. No piece of paper was going to erase Marcus from my world.

A few days later, I opened the box they gave me of Marcus's things. Damned if I didn't see that dress with the teal flowers on top.

I broke down, sobbing and buried my face in the cloth, wailing Marcus's name. My family watched speechless while I cried until it felt like my soul spilt out of me.

That night, I took the dress to bed and held it to my nose, trying to inhale the faintest smell of Marcus. I rubbed the flowers from the bridge of my nose over my lips and kissed them, then again from the bridge of my nose over my lips and kissed them.

God, why did you take Marcus away from me—from all of us?

I waited to hear something. To feel something. No answers came—just maybes. Maybe Marcus was never meant to go to war. Maybe his heart was too pure for this side of glory. Maybe Marcus was just on loan from heaven all along. But I discovered something I wouldn't have known had Marcus not come into my life. I discovered what love is and what it does. It hears my words and searches my thoughts. It never harms or humiliates; it holds and beholds beauty. Marcus sacrificed his life for me to live a better one. So, he has become the measure of love, the measure of my worth. And if none can love me as he had, then I'll remain his until God takes me, too.

TRANSCENDENCE

Section 5

TRANSCENDENCE

Elizabeth Best

Black women—deemed less than human—
breast-fed babies of plantation owners
who needed no reason to flay their bodies.
They packed salt and pepper
into the gaping flesh
with added spite.
Through tears,
ancestors saw freedom looming,
and so, on coral stones
of hard labor, men and women sharpened wit.
Left with determination to test the point and edge of it—
in the oppressors' native lands,
populated with opinions,
they marred migrants' lives with abrasive restrictions.

Ancestors flung against barriers
of hardcore prejudices

in church,
court,
school,
businesses
—forms of injustices
tough enough to notch the whetted blade
of common sense,
sharp enough to slice
decades of self-confidence.
Still, they established a legacy
built from daily acts of will
and bequeathed it to us
as this life-lasting and soul-saving skill—
the art of bending
beating
reshaping
all types of adversity until they transfigured
into novel forms of gainful opportunity.

In the colonizers' homelands,
folks viewed my ancestors
as weak
when they chose to turn scorched cheek
after cold-blasted cheek.
Yet, forebears worked overtime through hunger and sleeplessness
to polish divergent attitudes
and hone aptitudes to a fine keenness
against the flint-like expanse of widespread social inequity.
After slipping
        falling
on criticism's slope,
always chilly,

foreparents screwed their gumption and grit
to a sticking place
and built for descendants a solid,
heart-centered home base.

Legend says ancestors chanted *Irekoja*, *Irekoja*, *Irekoja*
and kept smiling
while within the depths
of each soul
the blues were wailing.
Voicing *Transcendence* in ancestral tongues
struck soul-oil,
a fuel refined from a blend of inspired will
and purposeful toil.
That energy drove Elders to be better, to achieve
much more than loved ones
who had slogged up Commitment Hill.
Powered by passion
and steered by a goal-driven self-manager,
ancestors cut and paved
wider paths for relatives who came later.

We, the offspring,
still trek
paths up
and down
Rejection Street.
Now, more doors open,
and more faces smile eager to greet us
as we enter to feed,
clean,
amuse young, ill, or aging folk

for whose kin we used to be the butt
of almost every racist joke.
As service providers in every former colonizing nation,
we still must fight daily
to secure our psycho-social emancipation
from generational traumas of self-hate and mental slavery, so we
still must pray for the liberation of haters from the hell of bigotry.

ON UNDERSTANDING THE PRESENCE OF GHOSTS

Odette Cortés

I remember the time I truly thought about the idea of a ghost and its repercussions in the world of the living. It was my freshman year of high school in Aguascalientes. For the first time in my life, I was enjoying a modicum of liberty, allowed to go to the movies with my friends—unsupervised. I had never watched a scary movie before, nor did I feel the desire to do so, but my mother misread my escape cues. I found myself in the movie theater undergoing a test of courage I undoubtedly failed. The movie was *The Ring*. The anticipation of the music scared me to death. Ashamed of the need to cover my eyes, I closed them without the aid of my hands, longing for the movie to be over. In the aftermath, I suffered a few days of sleeping with the lights on and a lifetime of avoiding scary movies. Back then, I failed the bravery test, but I am no longer afraid of ghosts.

Nowadays I think of ghosts all the time—maybe more about hauntings. By hauntings I mean events that have bled through the imaginary and appear. Events that are so traumatizing they leave a mark on the world's histories. These hauntings are retold, reimagined, rememorized in ways that create new horizons beyond the actual place of occurrence. I am not talking about a revamping of the story of a Japanese-inspired Western ghost, but rather about a sea of ghosts extending throughout the Atlantic.

Works of literature that have captured my attention share some things in common—the sea (the Middle Passage in particular) and ghosts that transit that space. Unlike the rage and vengefulness of Sadako, these restless ghosts are unable to haunt in, what we might call, a traditional way.

I am intrigued by M. NourbeSe Philip's take on the Zong massacre of 1781 and her need to "exhume" the bodies. Out of all the lingering tales of horror, this massacre exceeds all. A case tainted by legal vocabulary that strips every victim of humanity and even attempts to contest the fact they ever existed. About 150 enslaved Africans lost their lives on that ship. Legal documents only acknowledge that 132 were thrown overboard alive, those whose lives could be monetized as part of the insurance. Those who died of "natural" causes, or who dared to choose when to die, remain unaccounted for. Their bodies are lost to the Atlantic—their names, lost to the documents—their stories remain lost to us all. So, the atrocity they endured has become a haunting, making the sea, as Derek Walcott suggests, a place of history.

Now, we cannot fully lay these dead to rest as we do not know where they are or who they were. The traditional methods of bringing solace to the departed are rendered useless here. That is why Philip's idea of *exaqua*, the aquatic version of exhume, captures my imagination so violently. The nightmare of the Zong is unfathomable, surpassing anything I could imagine. Yet, countless have been, or are still, haunted by those events. They creep into our thoughts as evidence of the gruesomeness of the Middle Passage.

Performing an *exhaquation* is different for everyone. Rather than fixating on how the victims died, I wonder about their lives in Africa—their families, pets, and dreams. I think of them roaming the land, enveloped by loved ones, laughing. Unfortunately, these imaginings are but a sketch constructed by rough lines of what could have been. What did the survivors think and feel? If we have trouble laying to rest the events 200 years after its occurrence, what would it have been like to have witnessed them? Speaking about it would take time. First, to learn the new language, and then, how to articulate the level of horror. Would this be a story to my grandchildren? Is this a story I have to tell the world about?

With time, I have learned to carry these ghosts. Their haunting hauls a thirst for knowledge, a need to understand how such an atrocity could happen and how we can see that it never happens again. I am compelled to learn more about the past, about the Middle Passage, and the land that seems to be so far away from my home in Mexico. I carry this haunting, looking for my culture, little bits of Africa that have steadily been assimilated. I seek the apparitions left by the survivors in the beats of a *cumbión* or the notes of a *marimba*. The ghosts are not the scary beings that want to drag me into the spirit world, but are those wanting to be remembered, souls longing to be celebrated. I will welcome them to an altar on the next *Día de muertos* that they might visit, eat, and rest before they continue their journeys.

No. I am no longer afraid of ghosts.

TETHER

Nicole Negrón

Loiza stood silently in the glow of the Dollar Tree on Main Street. The store, like every other at this time, was closed, but the light from the bus station bounced in long swaths off the shops in the Wilkes-Barre town square. The quiet made Loiza shiver. There was no sign or sound of life. A single petal floated past her face and as she turned and reached up to finger the blooms on the flowering dogwood, a sticky red fingerprint appeared on the white petals. The contrast of the colors against each other intrigued the young woman, but did not raise her from her trance. Loiza looked down at her bloodied hands as a scream hot and liquid curled inside before finally escaping her throat. The deafening rattle punched her instincts into overdrive as she looked around for witnesses. Two college boys came sprinting around the corner.

"You okay," one of the young men asked, looking for danger. Loiza looked down to find herself clean of the blood. Her face burned with shame at having cried wolf.

Loiza's eyes darted from the boy in savior mode to the other one. She felt her brownness as his blue eyes crawled over her body with a glimmer of lust. Goosebumps rose on her deep brown skin with the claws of his desire tearing at her dress. Her great grandmother's words echoed in her mind, "Your skin is the kiss of God, makes it a beacon to the devil." The fear and pride of her namesake in their African roots was superimposed over her entire life.

"*Ta bien*," Loiza said as she sped past the men and in the direction of the bar. She could not remember how she arrived downtown, or when. Still in a bit of a daze, she thanked her ancestors for the sprinkling of clarity that carried her towards the crowded scene. Throngs of college students in high heels and unbuttoned shirts made her feel twice the age of 25. Loiza had never felt comfortable at bars, and she couldn't place a single face in the crowd.

She remembered her phone, purse, and smartwatch—all curiously absent. The strong scent of cedarwood tickled her nose as she felt someone brush hard against her backside. Loiza stifled the urge to vomit as her eyes met the stranger pushing up against her.

"You're pretty for a Black girl," he said, "You must be mixed."

Loiza quickly turned away, but a group of young women laughing and shrieking stood between her and escape. She pushed through the mob of street drinkers, then through the dancing, to the bar. Loiza waited twenty minutes through music bouncing from rap to techno, the sexual tension of the dance floor, men hitting on her, the whooping and hollering of college cliques.

"What can I get for you?" asked the bartender.

A woman stood at least 6'3, towering, but elegant, with long, dark hair waving down past her shoulders. Loiza winced at first sight of her irisless eyes and translucent skin. She wore a long sleeve, spandex crop top and shimmering overalls. One strap hung from the silver overalls, and the bouncing laser lights made her glow prismatically.

"You okay?" the bartender asked.

"*Necessito*," Loiza stopped to clear her throat and calm herself. She tried again, but her broken Spanish was all that emerged from her mouth. Loiza ran the words through her head once more, then raised her voice over the music. "Has anyone returned a purse, phone, keys, um anything. I, um, can't find my things."

The bartender eyed Loiza, then disappeared to the other end of the bar.

Loiza let out a defeated sigh. She was stranded without her wallet and keys. *Oh God*, she thought. *Someone might have my address—and the keys to get in.* She suddenly became aware of the mounting perspiration on her upper lip and forehead, of her heartbeat accelerating. Just as panic began to boil up from her gut, she heard someone clear their throat behind her.

"This yours?" the bartender asked.

Loiza simply nodded.

"What's in it?" The question seemed merely a formality.

"Um… my wallet, my ID, keys…"

The bartender tossed the small purse onto the bar and walked away. Loiza snatched the satchel and made a beeline for the door. Still confused as to why and how she'd gotten there, she briskly walked out of the bar and across the street to the small center of the downtown area. She needed to escape the music and busyness of the bar but was too afraid to be completely alone and out of sight. After calling up an Uber, she secretly counted the cash in her wallet. Something niggled at her, but she wasn't sure what. She looked down at her phone: *11:07 p.m.*

As Loiza grew closer to home, anticipation formed in her belly. She pumped her hands in and out of nervous fists, and her eyes clambered over every centimeter of the dark. Her subconscious searched for something her body knew to fear. The air conditioner of the Ford Taurus blasted shivers onto her skin, and yet sweat continued to flood her every surface. She found herself, unwittingly, flapping the neckline of her dress for relief from the burn of the unknowable fear. *You're fine,* she thought to herself as she gripped and released the backseat.

A brilliant white cross came into focus at the top of the church steeple, having a veiled sense of familiarity, safety, and fear in its shadow. Loiza thought of the bartender. The image and shadow were simply a flicker as the car seemed to move faster down the road.

"It's just up the road here. You'll miss it if you don't—," she began, but the clock on the radio blinked.

"1:29 a.m.," Loiza whispered.

"I've never missed it," the driver said, smiling before turning the display off.

Loiza stopped breathing.

The corner of the old factory-turned-apartment-building sat neatly off the street, almost hiding behind the Russian Orthodox church. Her temporary home's muck-brown color typically blended into the night, but a shining *something* illuminated the three-step entrance.

Loiza yelled, "Go," but the car crawled to a stop. Her head snapped from the illumination to the front of the car that now sat empty. Before she could question the driver's disappearance, the bright source evaporated into an opening.

A rising and steady sound emitted from the opening. Loiza instantly recognized the thrum of the *buleador*, the alternating slap and open tone, steady and unyielding. Her feet slow at first, but not precautious, carried her from the empty car. Then she heard it, the soft clicking of the *cua*, snapping her head to the right. To the left she heard the *shoosh* and *shuck* of the maracas. All at once, Loiza sprinted toward the opening, responding to the call of the *laina*. Carried into the opening by her ancestors, Loiza disappeared from the street, and the light followed.

As she moved through the light, Loiza's legs rose from underneath her. A shroud of white slowly engulfed them, then her torso. The fear of the night melted away as she landed with a soft thud on her bare feet. Her eyes did not open, but her heartbeat slowed to match the thrum of the *buleador*. With closed eyes, she saw the beautiful men in their buttoned *guayaberas*, a second layer of white linen and buttoned to the top despite the heat. Her skin felt melted, hot and marvelous.

And the music. She recognized it, and it recognized her. It curled over her feet and up her legs, dragging her hands onto her face. The white swath of muslin wrapped around her ears and tied at the top of her forehead. Her curly hair now swooped up into a pineapple. She didn't open her eyes but could see a stout woman crouched low, hands gripping the middle of her skirts and petticoats as she walked the *paseo*, the circular path, saluting the *buleador*. Then, the *piquetes* and the *marullos*. The woman swung her arms and skirts from side to side. No words uttered as the jerking and unpredictable movements of her feet, shoulders, and waist elicited the reaction of the drums… and her heart. The woman turned to face her, and finally, Loiza opened her eyes.

The others slowly accompanied the woman. All of their bodies seemed to sing, to belt, to pound. And the leader's eyes said it all. Only she, clad in her white shirtwaist and long skirts, could see Loiza. She beckoned her near. In unison, their shoulders bucked and spread. The drums and the women and the small crowd acknowledged and retorted their movements. In unison, their arms flapped as Loiza mimicked the *paseo*, then the *abanico doble*, quick stepping and remembering…

Why are you so angry?
Why are you so loud?
You don't look Puerto Rican.
You must be mixed.
You must be mixed.

Those words didn't even make her the angriest, yet they bounced off the chambers of her mind. And as the words echoed for a third time, a slap of the drums replaced them until nothing was in her mind. Nothing but the creases in the corners of her great grandmother's smiling eyes. Nothing but the curve of her mother's mouth as she tastes the labor of her time in the kitchen. And with the joy that seemed to erupt under her feet so too came the tender inkling of something she had never felt. As the earth made its presence known, her mind almost named the thing.

Then, she heard it. The processional's song.

"*O Mar. El mar es una mujer. Ella nos trajo aqui. Ella nos llevo a una libertad.*"

The sea is a woman. She carried us here. She carried us here to a freedom.

And with that last word, her third eye opened. Her feet slowed in tandem with the others as they circled the path first set by the *laina*. Loiza caught her breath, and the outline of the setting formed as if drawn, shaded, then colored. Each of the last steps pulsed life into the scene before her, and as she swung her arms and head in either direction, she came to understand where she was. *Puerto Rico, but when*?

Finally, the drummers and the dancers smiled and laughed and clapped their hands together. The sounds of love and comradery made Loiza smile until she remembered—she was invisible. Here, too, as in life, she was not a part of the joy, the party, the group. She was invisible. The thought almost dampened her spirits, but the scene unfolding before her was too vibrant and lively.

In quick succession the street and small, windowless *bohios* flickered to life. The modest abodes made of wood and dried palm fronds buzzed with laughing porch dwellers. The mussed dirt roads, a dusty fury of passersby—women and children and men. Some underdressed for outside and some overdressed for the heat, but jovial, taking notice of the newly dismembering crowd of dancers and musicians. Loiza took note of the various languages being spoken, mixed into the same conversations. She tried to make sense of it all. *1800s*?

"Mar," she heard someone call out.

Loiza turned her head in tandem. Mar was her great-great-grandmother's name, and looking upon the countenance of the woman, the *laina* she knew—somehow—had drawn her there. She recognized the almond eyes, broad mouth, and pronounced jawline of the matriarch she had only seen in photos. The woman, Mar, turned to respond to her friend, then looked back over her shoulder. Loiza almost missed it—the slight wink and curve of Mar's grin.

As Loiza followed her ancestor through the small, seaside town, she drank in every sign of the time. The various African flags, happy but worn-down inhabitants, and the scent of it all—the spices, the sweat, the *sopas*, and rice. Between the bare feet of the laughing children, and the over-necked blouses tucked into flowing skirts, Loiza's family came to mind.

"*Que rico, heh*," Mar said without turning to Loiza, seeming to realize her presence.

Loiza couldn't muster a response. Her mind was too full now; her senses overloaded. Instead, she just mumbled, *Mm*.

When the two arrived at Mar's home, the door was ajar and Loiza could hear whining and chatting from inside. The small home was full of young women: some cleaning up, others hanging about on the sparse furniture, and the source of the whining. Mar greeted each woman—Alma, Abeni, Maria, Ife, and the whiner—Enitan.

"You bringing ghosts in here with you again?" Alma asked, getting up to leave. Mar shot her a smirk but didn't answer.

"Abeni, *mi amor*, what are you doing to *pobre* Enitan?" Mar asked mockingly.

Enitan sucked her teeth and rolled her eyes, which elicited a brush smack in the head from Abeni. Abeni sat at the edge of the cattail leaf chair with Enitan between her legs, enduring the yanking, hitting, combing, and braiding.

"Sit still, *nina*," Mar said, laughing as the girl winced.

When Enitan sucked at her teeth again, Abeni warned, "She the reason you here. The reason you free. Forget again, and I'll give you more than a *cocotaso*."

At that, the women laughed heartily. Mar brought a glass jar of something mud-colored and thick over to Abeni, pointing with pinched lips at Enitan's head. Half of her thick wool hair was knotted at the top of her head while Abeni tried in vain to pass a brush through chunks of it at a time. Despite the pattern of separating and yanking, the young girl seemed giddy at the prospect of Mar's concoction.

"You have beautiful hair. You can thank Mar for that, too," Abeni started to say, but Mar cut her off.

"*Tss*. All she can thank me for is less dryness. Every beautiful thing she got, 'specially that hair, came from her ancestors," Mar said sternly. Abeni simply nodded. And as Abeni fingered small amounts of the moisturizer onto the younger girl's head—the edges along her forehead and in between the parts—Loiza's feet began to tingle. The feeling became stronger until she could no longer take it and looked down.

She found herself sitting on the packed dirt floor, legs folded and growing numb. The cool, damp dirt brought things into focus. Her head yanked to the side, and she looked up and saw Abeni, her face solemn as she carefully pulled apart a small section of hair. Abeni smiled at Loiza and patted her shoulder, then continued. Loiza felt the depression of Abeni's index finger lightly push into her scalp, the musky smell of the moisturizer tingled in her nose and on her skin. Then she felt the soft, tight pulls of her strands being intertwined.

All the while, Mar stood by an open fire pit, stirring and dropping things into a large kettle. She hummed something bass-y and rambling as her hips swayed. For the first time in a long time, Loiza felt like—home.

Mar turned to look at her and winked.

"*Finito*," Adeni said as she tapped Loiza's head and nudged her out of the way.

Adeni chuckled and disappeared outside with the other women. Loiza reached up to feel her tendrils wrapped into one long braid around her head like a crown. She smiled through the pain.

Mar crossed to the part of the room that served as a kitchen to hang her apron. Near the latch, a billhook stood propped in the corner. Mar paused, staring at it momentarily, then suddenly Loiza saw a raised billhook in the flashes of her mind.

Instantly, a burning sensation spread from her neck, skin to muscles. Loiza moved to rub it when she felt the weight of the billhook in her hands. The ache and burn of a long day's work screamed through her arms as she tried to use her forearm to shield her eyes from the sun. The merciless sun was only rivaled by the stare of an overseer, stomping through the sugar cane, through the rows of toiling folk, squatting and bent over, swinging their arms to cut and pry the damned things from a 6-inch height. Loiza quickly averted her eyes as the overseer's shadow engulfed her. Unused to the burden of the squat, bend, and yank, her muscles seized up. Her skin burned with each cramp. The sweat cascaded down her face and arms, the moisture a stinging bath. She kept her head down, but let her eyes shift around the hellish field. Just as the overseer turned back in her direction, Loiza's knees seized and released. She was saved by a young man with long, fine tendrils flowing loosely down the length of his back who cried out and dropped to his knees at the same moment.

Instinctively, his arm flew up to block the coming whip. A large bleeding gash appeared in his hand and the blood was so perfuse, it showered his copper skin.

"*Limpiar eso, y trabaja*," the overseer screamed, but the man made no motion to move. "*Ahora*!"

The young man placed his hands onto his thighs and let his head hang down as he kneeled. His back heaved as he took several deep breaths. Some of the folks kept working. Others looked on with mixed emotions, taking advantage of the scene unfolding before them, to have a much-needed break.

Loiza locked eyes with Mar, younger and with a slightly swollen belly, but Loiza recognized her instantly. Mar stared hard at the young man. Her face was covered in sweat and tears, and a look of desperation. Loiza looked away, squeezed her eyes shut, then looked back. Instead of Mar, her eyes locked onto the man, then she felt it—the extraordinary pang of despair, fatigue, pride, and anger, a different kind of ache.

A scream snapped her to, and she looked up just in time to see the snap and slice of the whip across the young man's back.

"Aguey!" Loiza yelled out.

Then, someone in the distance yelled, "Agueybana!"

Another snap and slice, and another until a bell rang out. With their heads low, the field's inhabitants slowly filed away. Only Loiza, Abeni, Alma, Maria, and Ife remained. The women helped lower Loiza to her knees, though Agueybana refused to look up at her. She reached out for him, and his reluctance made her take hold of his chin. As she lifted his face, his tears and defiance melted into shame. He understood that his actions had condemned them both.

Loiza pulled his broken body into her arms. The women looked down the expanse of the field, praying in different languages. Loiza and Agueybana sobbed, her tears setting his open wounds aflame.

Once home, Mar took to making the salve for her husband's wounds. Loiza watched as her ancestor gathered various plant cuttings into the *pilon*.

"And for good measure," Mar whispered in Loiza's direction before praying, then spitting into it.

Loiza looked at Agueybana, who stared directly at her with fear.

Sensing Loiza's confusion, Mar whispered, "I fear this means he's close to death." Then, to her husband, "She is our great, great."

This made the man smile, and Mar turned, concealing her tears.

When Mar moved towards her husband, Maria busted in, prompting Abeni to emerge from the other room.

"Something's happened," Maria said.

"You go," Mar replied, pushing Abeni towards the door.

Several men and women huddled around a makeshift storefront. A young boy sat on a stool with an elderly woman standing behind him. He silently read a tattered piece of paper as the others stood in anticipation.

"What else it say, *nino*?" someone asked.

"So, far it say we free," someone else whispered.

Loiza could feel the crowd's anticipation rumbling like a storm cloud. She held her breath.

"Spanish Army, born after 1868, *y* the *viejos*," the boy read.

The last declaration garnered teeth sucking from a few in the crowd and a slap in the back of the head from the women standing next to him.

The boy added, "Suppose who has it can buy their freedom."

Abeni threw her hands up and slumped back toward Mar.

"Some freed. Nothing that applies to us. 'Less you have *dinero* stashed I don't know about," she said.

Agueybana looked up at his wife, then quickly averted his eyes.

"Thank you, Abeni. You should head home. It's late," she replied.

Once Abeni had gone, Agueybana said shamefully, "they'll never let us free now."

"All they care about is dinero. Trick is—how we ask to be freed without saying we want to be freed," Mar said.

"*Tu marido. Donde esta*," the overseer yelled into the back of Mar's head.

Mar was about to answer when she felt the communion of Loiza's essence. All at once, she looked upon her physical self. Loiza embodied her, and while a part of Mar was frightened by what that meant, another felt the lull of the spiritual world and the peace of being rid of the physical one. Though Mar hovered beside her corporeal self, a tether kept her from being swept away.

Loiza's spirit warmed at the gift of peace she lent her ancestor, but a sharp pain in her calf brought her down hard onto the left knee.

"*Tu marido*," the overseer repeated, having just kicked her.

"Only be a burden here, them whips on," Loiza began to say, when Abeni interrupted.

"We, two, make enough for the three of us."

"We three," Maria chimed in.

The overseer studied the three women, then Mar's belly. He sucked his teeth and walked away. As he sauntered in the other direction, Maria helped Loiza to her feet.

"Chica, what was that?"

Unsure of what to say, Loiza simply groaned, picked up her billhook, and began to work again.

For a week, Loiza awoke in Mar's body to toil in the heat and dirt; the unfamiliar weight of life growing in her and bearing down on her every joint and muscle. For a week, Loiza felt the turmoil of peace and pain. *When will this end? What's my purpose here?* On the seventh day, she heard the words Mar had longed to hear.

"He's gone," the folks in the field whispered.

Before Loiza dared ask who, she saw someone slowly galloping through the field on a tall horse. She stood taller than any man, having long dark hair and eyes that seemed irisless. The new overseer was a woman.

"Since when they let their women work?" someone whispered.

"And in the fields at that," another said.

The new overseer sauntered along the hushed chorus. She looked ahead and above the folks in the field until she spied Mar and her visibly puffed belly.

"You there," she said in a raised voice, but no one wanted to be the "you" she was referring to. She galloped to Loiza. "*Hablas ingles*?"

"Yes," Loiza replied in a meek voice. After a week of heat, bend, swipe, Loiza didn't want to cause any more damage to her ancestor's physical form.

"Go get a drink of water," the woman said from her horse.

"It's… it's not time, yet," Loiza replied.

"It's time when I say it's time. Everyone, go get a drink, a quick drink."

No one hesitated, but no one dared to run either. As Loiza moved to follow the others, the woman blocked her way with the horse. She jumped down in one swift motion that made Loiza wince.

"Buy your freedom, *nina*," the woman whispered, then leaned over and said something else only Loiza and Mar's spirit could hear. Though delighted within, Loiza simply nodded at the woman with a solemn face.

At the end of the workday, Loiza rushed ahead of her friends. With each stride closer to home, Loiza felt music inside her. Just when she thought her feet might carry her into a dance, her chest tightened, and Mar's essence ripped her from the body. Mar knew something she couldn't share, but Loiza could feel it—terror.

Mar broke into a run. Her eyes stung with tears and sweat. The muscles of her feet screamed for relief and her knees felt as if they would collapse upon themselves, but she ran. Villagers jumped out of her way in disdain and curiosity. Abeni and Maria trailed far behind, but they, too, started to run. Loiza felt a rush of confusion and fear and… dissolution from her tether with her ancestor and with the place. She felt porous, and the wind began to pass through pockets of her body. Her feet no longer touched the floor, and just when she thought she'd disappear forever, back to her time or back to nowhere, she passed through the door of Mar's home.

Loiza watched helplessly as Mar dropped to her knees and raised Agueybana's lifeless body in her arms. Then, Loiza found herself sobbing onto his face. Her body was awash with his blood, and she could feel the last of his life being carried away with it. The ache of Mar's heart sent a shockwave over Loiza's essence. The tether between her and this world faded. She reached up, trying to grab hold of something, anything. She couldn't leave Mar now. *Please God. Not now.*

"I don't want to go," Loiza cried out. "Don't make me leave her."

She looked around for Mar's spirit, but could see nothing except blood. Loiza gripped Agueybana's body tighter until he turned into a bright burst of light that leapt from his body like a flare, pausing for a second before disappearing. In the same moment, Loiza found herself standing over Mar's body, engulfing her, as her ancestor prayed.

Mar said a prayer for Agueybana, and for their unborn child, then for herself. Then, she looked into Loiza's eyes and said a prayer for her, too. And something called to Mar, and Loiza also heard it. The *laina*. The *bomba* music called to them both, but Mar could not answer and so Loiza could not.

And when another seven days passed, seven days of visits to the sobbing, bed-stricken Mar, seven days of meals, and prayers, and love, the *laina* called again. Loiza answered them both. And in the reply of her *paseo* and her *abanico doble*, and the buck and spread of her shoulders and arms, she prayed. Loiza prayed to take the pain of her ancestors with her. With that prayer, every void filled with it, the pain wrapped and beamed with the work, the love, and the triumph of them all. And one by one, the people of Loiza, Puerto Rico, stood and looked up to see her fleeting spirit.

THE GREAT STONE

Yakhare Gueye

The moon peaked through the clouds in the darkness of the night. It gave little light to the expansive space yet cast a shimmering gleam on the green crystal stone that dominated the room.

Kaabo longed for the nights to come—when visitors left the exhibit, exiting the double doors of the Museum of Plymouth. The security guard with the shiny bald head peeked into the room, quickly surveyed it, then shut the wooden doors behind him. Kaabo waited for the sound of his heavy boots and clanging keys to grow fainter before she'd finally get to wipe her arm on something—anything.

Early that afternoon, a ginger boy reached over the red rope and "DO NOT TOUCH" sign with a mysteriously wet hand. He wiped it on her arm and giggled like he was keeping a secret. He then looked around the crowded room to make sure no one was watching before hovering his other hand over the carved sword she held. None of the tourists saw what he did, but he wasn't the only one who knew his little secret. As his fingers grazed the edge of the sword, he looked up and made direct eye contact with Kaabo. Her eyes were once staring straight ahead, but now glared right into the boy's sweaty, red tinted face.

Kaabo wanted to slap the boy for touching her precious weapon, but when he screamed and ran out of the room, she barely kept her composure. As the hours passed, the presence of the peculiar liquid on her arm irritated her. So, the first thing she did when the double doors to the African Exhibit were slammed shut—after her arms, legs, neck, and head transformed from marble into smooth brown skin—was wipe her arm on her wrapper.

"What part of 'do no touch' don't people understand?" she muttered as the other surrounding statues began to unfreeze.

"I know," said Yata with the zig-zag cornrows. She grabbed her throat, gagging, "A lady had her face so close to mine and her breath reeked of fish."

"Could have been worse," the honey-beige girl teased as she stretched out her limbs. "Remember the boy who bit into my leg?"

Kaabo barked out a laugh at the memory of the face that Niatou made when it happened but was quickly interrupted by a gruff voice.

"Kaabo, it is your turn to stay here and watch over the Great Stone," said Louk. He was the oldest of them, an umber-skinned man with gray streaked braids. Kaabo bit her tongue and managed to nod instead. She watched in envy as the rest of the Askugo walked to the door before Yata pried it open with her shining green rope. The sound of their slapping bare feet grew quieter as Kaabo was left alone in the empty room—save for the green crystal that attracted people from all over the world to see up close. She sheathed her sword and circled the crystal once, twice, then three times before sitting beside it.

Kaabo traced the patterns on her wrapper. Flowers and geometric shapes in dark, earthy colors outlined the cloth, having green streaks as bright as the stone. She sighed, tracing the lines over and over again, growing more bored with every passing second. She occupied herself, remembering times before she was brought to the museum; memories of loved ones who were left behind.

While the others explored the rest of the museum, Kaabo was stuck on patrol. There's not much she can really do when she and the rest of the Askugo are stuck in this building for days and days. They can't even stray far from the gem that was once buried on their land's soil without turning into permanent stone.

Kaabo placed her cheek on the crystal that pulsed with heat. She grazed it with her long fingers like she had hundreds of times before. The comforting warmth made her eyes droop, but they flew open when she saw movement from the corner of them.

She quickly rose to her feet, her heart pumping faster. Her eyes darted all over the room while she paced around the stone. Her bare feet stopped suddenly, and she held her breath, waiting to hear something. There was no sound nor movement.

Kaabo breathed in deeply, ready to exhale, when the breath was knocked out of her. She was suddenly slammed against the crystal. Her neck and shoulder ached, but she still managed to whip her head up. She gasped at the sight of a person atop of the stone, dressed in a black cloak and ski mask.

Kaabo unshielded her sword with its leather hilt, the body glittered green as the stone. She gripped it tight before climbing the crystal with one hand, her breath growing heavy. She quickly reached the trespasser, crying out as she swiped at their leg.

The intruder dodged the swipe, stumbling back as Kaabo swiped the other leg while dangling from the stone's edge. She pulled herself up with one arm before standing in front of them. Without a moment to catch her breath, she jabbed at the unwelcomed guest again and again, but they repeatedly avoided the moves. If they hadn't leapt back when she sliced at their chest, then she would've immediately finished them off.

Kaabo sliced open the front of the cloak, hearing a gruff groan, and revealing a pale white chest. *Of course.*

She angled her sword to strike again but flinched when the man quickly retrieved something from inside his cloak. Kaabo should have been unfazed that he wielded his own weapon, but her hand flew over her mouth at the sight of *what* he held.

Kaabo had seen European weapons up close from previous intruders, but she never saw anyone hold a glittering green sword of their own. The sight of it made her head spin, but she screamed aloud when the man swung down at the stone and took out a big chunk of it.

The stone shook from the impact and the thief kicked at Kaabo's stomach, sending her flying. Her back hit the ground, and she wheezed, seeing stars dance in her vision. When she looked up, the person was gone, having chopped an animal-sized chunk off of the stone.

Before Kaabo could rise to her feet, the rest of the Askugo stormed in. They gasped at the broken gem, some with bulging eyes, others placing their hands on their heads. Louk marched over to Kaabo and yanked her from the ground by her shoulders. He said nothing for a while, but his bushy furrowed eyebrows did all the talking.

"Kaabo, Kaabo what happened?" he spat as his eyes jumped from the stone to Kaabo's sweaty face.

"…Someone came in," she swallowed. "He wore all black and came out of nowhere. He had the exact same weapon as mine—made out of the Great Stone!"

The others grew quiet, some faces filled with fear, while others seemed angry and betrayed.

"Kaabo, why didn't you stop them," Louk said slowly, his tone growing angrier by the second.

"What?" she balked. "I did try!" Kaabo turned to the rest of the Askugo who appeared not to believe her. "Are you guys really blaming me?" Sweat leaked into her eyes as tears threatened to cloud her vision.

"There was no way someone could come in here. Waraba and Niatou were at the door and saw nothing. Look me in my eyes and tell me—"

"You can't blame me for this!" Kaabo yelled, wiping her face and whipping her head towards the others. Kaabo shivered at the thought of talking to an elder like this, but her anger and heartache seized control of any sense she had left.

"Even if someone did come," Louk continued, "we know you are capable of defeating them. Did you really let them go? Did you instead take—"

"Why would I take it!" Kaabo's right temple pounded as she grits her teeth. "Where's the missing chunk if I did take it, Uncle?"

Louk scanned her up and down before turning away, suggesting he was done with the conversation. But Kaabo wasn't. She grabbed his wrist and stumbled in front of him before trying to defend herself once again.

"Uncle—all of you—you have to believe me!" Tears were now falling from Kaabo's face. She wiped it once again. "A white man came out of nowhere with the same weapon as I had! He was the one who took a chunk out of the Great Stone! You have to—" Kaabo looked into the elder's dark eyes, now surrounded by more wrinkles, and she knew he didn't believe a word she said.

Louk nearly whispered, "Are you working with the white man, Kaabo?"

She wanted to defend herself, to prove her innocence, but now struggled to get any words pass her trembling lips. "Why would I do that?" she croaked.

"Same reason why the Great Stone was taken in the first place," he seethed, the words stabbing her chest like daggers. "You were easily bribed by the white man, charmed by their gifts in exchange for access to the stone.

"When we were brought here, we gave an oath to protect the Great Stone. Yet you didn't do that." He glanced at Yata who gripped her rope—the same rope used to trap intruders and get rid of traitors.

Kaabo stepped back as she slowly raised her sword, wiping at her face. Yata avoided Kaabo's eyes, staring at the rope held tightly in her palms. When Yata took a step forward, Kaabo took one back and gripped her sword tighter. She knew what would happen. Her own people were going to kick her out, and she will stay frozen if she remains far from the stone.

They blamed her, but it was the white man who did it. The same people took the Great Stone before, causing everyone back home to turn into stone. These also took her and a few other Askugo to be used as tourist attractions. They tore them away from their land and was now tearing her away from the last people she had left.

When Yata finally looked up at Kaabo, her eyes screamed an apology, but a booming voice from the back of the crowd broke the silence.

"Baba, you cannot be serious," a voice said. When Kaabo looked at the owner of the cry, it belonged to Louk's grandson Zir, a usually quiet young man with coffee-toned skin and a head of thick coily hair. Zir and Kaabo had once been close, but he hadn't said a word to her since they were brought the museum years ago.

"Baba, you do realize that if you kick her out, she'll be stuck until the day she dies?" Zir said. Kaabo grew nervous for Zir as he confronted the elder in her defense. Louk glared back at him, a glare that could make a child cry.

"Yes, I am aware," Louk spat. "But what difference does it make? There's thousands of our people back home who are frozen because there's no stone with them! I cannot sit here and let her endanger us any longer." Louk's voice began strong yet wavered by the finish of his sentence.

"This is different though," Zir said, glancing at Kaabo's wet face before turning back to Louk. "If you kick her out, you will be just as bad as the people who took the Great Stone from us. At least let her redeem herself."

Silence stretched out for a few, tensed-filled seconds before Zir continued, "If she can prove that it was someone attacking the stone, then she stays, and we figure out a way to prevent the real offenders from coming back for more. If not, then you do whatever you want."

"No—" Louk began before Zir cut him off again.

"Please?"

Louk sucked his teeth, giving in to his son before walking towards the stone. He examined it before sitting on the ground in front of it. The others followed while eyeing Kaabo with accusing stares. Despite the rest of her people surrounding her from all around, Kaabo felt very alone.

Guilt weighed down on her chest as she blinked away tears. Kaabo grew angry at herself for crying in the first place. It was same guilt she felt years ago when watching the white men steal the Great Stone after she naively led them to it. She watched everyone around her turn into stone in the hours that it was taken from the land. She and a few others were shoved into a dark ship, and her companions cried and screamed when brought into this room for the first time—being confused, lost, homesick—scared.

The first time was a mistake. But as Kaabo sat curled into a corner of the room, she swore to prove herself. As she looked into the stressed faces of her fellow Askugo, she decided she would find the person who stole from them and prove her innocence.

Kaabo looked up at the bright green crystal with a new resolve. She would do the impossible and bring her people back home with the Great Stone in tow.

COULD'VE

Akin Jeje

If we could've improve the past,
Robert Nesta Marley would still be singings songs of freedom,
an'
Zimbabwe would truly be free.

If we had disproved the past,
Gangs and drugs would have zipped by,
Fast,
All our youth gassed on graduate degrees.

We have not completely failed the aspirations
Of our parents, many now deceased,
With professions, families and properties,
Yet beyond is the Promised Land,
As we wander through Nomadlands,
Nomanslands,
Decades past our King's prophetic decree.

We strive to be,
But what are we, but awash
In the acrid bitterness of history?
Our Passover
Is adorned by the bricks and mortar
We built for others. Astringent herbs
We savor, milling miles through deserts
Falling prodigal to golden idols.
Will fatted calves still await
Our arrival?

I plead guilty to charges criminal and uncivil
That I have underserved the people.
My selfishness and short sight
Has wreaked an existential blight.

We were a generation borne into frustration.
Too many expired long before retirement.
Even away from strife of the streets, we were rafters,
Rife with disease, fruits of overwork, leisure without relief,
Lesser idols than Whitney, Prince and Michael
Fervent figures skating over a bottomless grief.
Turned back on the TV,
Innocent lad, black, wrong address,
Blasted twice, bitter relic, white,
In Kansas City, Missouri.

Further north,
Chi-Town last week,
Thousands of the youth dem,
Burned, bashed, twerked, blazed and blazed
Most everything,
In desperate pursuit of release.

It could've been better,
It could've always been more,
Than this.
What is it now,
What is it here,
That
We actually achieved?

CONTRIBUTORS

& ACKNOWLEDGEMENTS

BLACK DIASPORA

Bello Abdullahi, author of "10,000 Bullets," is from Abuja, Nigeria. He is a physics and computer science teacher and "all-around tech guy" who also loves writing in his spare time. Abdullahi wrote the novels *Dream Generation*, a compelling narrative addressing HIV/AIIDS awareness and *Lord of the Sea: Genies of Angass*, a captivating African fantasy tale.

Margaret Ajakaiye, a British Nigerian writer, creates across various genres. She placed as a finalist in *Kinsman Quarterly's* 2023 African Diaspora Award with her captivating poetry collection, "Cautious Incarceration" where she confronts time, love, and the pain of expectations. Ajakaiye has a Bachelor's and Master's degree in civil engineering and enjoys writing poetry, painting and dancing in her free time.

Elizabeth Best, poet of "Black Love Unspoken" and "Transcendence," lives in Louisville, Kentucky. She has been teaching language arts for the past 20 years and is a former linguistics lecturer for the University of the West Indies (UWI). Best won 2nd place in the Frogmore Poetry Contest and 3rd Place in the Caribbean Magazine Plus Contest. She has also been published in the *Courier Journal* (Louisville) and has a published collection, called *Barbed Wire & Roses*.

Tiara Imani Blain, MA, author of "From Sacred Lands To Fragile Seas," writes various forms of scientific/technical content related to physical and mental health, lifestyle, and health equity. Since age 11, she has indulged in writing short stories, poetry, and children's books. Her artistic endeavors include cinematography and digital illustration. Blain is also passionate about producing technical and creative content for communities with less access to such information.

Carmen Brady-Bronston, poet of "The Pilgrim's Rest," completed her undergraduate degree in biochemistry and molecular biology, yet followed her passion for story, earning her Masters of Arts in creative writing at Dartmouth College. She now lives in Dallas-Forth Worth with her husband and son. Her appreciation for family inspired her most recent publication, *Call of the Song Sparrow: A Novel.*

Nikę Campbell, the Nigerian-American author of "The Silent Passenger," won second-place for the African Diaspora Award. She grew up in Lagos, Nigeria, and currently lives in Florida with her family. Campbell also wrote the novels, *Thread of Gold Beads* and *Saro*. She was a finalist of the 2018 Red Hen Press Fiction Award for her historical fiction manuscript while several of her short stories from the collection, *Bury Me Come Sunday Afternoon,* were adapted for an award-winning film.

Odette Cortés, author of "On Understanding the Presence of Ghosts," lives in Mexico City as a graduate student at Universidad Nacional Autónoma de México where she also teaches in the undergraduate program. Her field of research is Caribbean literature and diaspora. She enjoys knitting, drawing, and writing across multiple genres, especially in poetry.

Charmaine Denison-George, creator of "Impedimenta," is from Freetown, Sierra Leone. She is a candidate for an MFA in creative writing at Texas State University and enjoys writing fiction, nonfiction, poetry, and occasionally serves as an associate editor at *Poda-Poda Stories*, a Sierra Leonean literary organization. Denison-George's work has appeared in *Brittle Paper* and *Isele Magazine*.

Monique Franz, author of "Kinda Green, Kinda Blue," is the senior editor for *Kinsman Quarterly*. The short story was among her first as a creative writing graduate student at Wilkes University, where she earned a Master of Fine Arts in creative writing. She has multiple publications as a published journalist and playwright. Her latest work is *Legacy of a Father*, a series of one-act plays inspired by interviews of individuals raised without a father's love.

Sophia Obianamma Gabriel created the fiction piece, "Hold My Broken Boy Together." She lives in Nigeria and is a poet and writer of family, romance, and horror stories. She is a student at the College of Nursing and Midwifery and also serves as an intern with *Kinsman Quarterly's* editing team. Gabriel published "When Food = Love" in the Brittle Paper Festive Anthology of 2022. She further published *Queen of Atregin*, *A Toy Story (House of Horrors)*, and *The Colour of Desire*.

Yakhare Gueye, author of "The Great Stone," is a recent recruit on the journalist team for *Kinsman Quarterly* and a general studies major at the Community College of Baltimore County. She plans to transfer as a Business Communications major with a minor in English. Her hobbies include reading and writing science fiction and fantasy, watching TV/ anime, and spending time with her Senegalese family.

Akin Jeje, creator of "Could've," is a Nigerian-Canadian poet with work featured internationally. He is the literature director for *Kinsman Quarterly* and a regular contributor to *Cha: An Asian Literary Journal*. His first collection, *Smoked Pearl*, was published in 2010 and long listed for the 2009 International Proverse Prize. Other works include, "Ping Shan Heritage Trail" in the *WHERE ELSE: An International Hong Kong Poetry Anthology* (April 2023) and the full poetry manuscript, *write about here*.

Veripuami Nandee Kangumine authored the poetry collection "The Loneliness of Shadows." She is a Namibian poet and writer whose poetry will soon appear in the anthology, "My Heart in your Hand" and *Doek Literary Magazine* (2020) and *Isele Magazine*. She was selected in *Islele's Magazine* as one of the Young Ten African Poets to watch in 2021.

.

Kay Lopez lives in the UK, but was born and raised in Kenya. She is passionate about telling the stories of her community, such as in her work, "Illness and Slow Food," published by *Kinsman Quarterly*. The essay is a parable about the process of grief understood in the preparation of a traditional home-cooked stew.

Hadija Mude, another native of Kenya, resides in Florida and is among the top finalists of the African Diaspora Award. Her short story, *Living Water*, is a captivating tale of a daughter's love for her mother and provides social commentary about the impact of political corruption upon a land's most vulnerable residents. Besides writing short literary fiction, Mude's hobbies include reading and traveling.

Nicole Negrón, author of "Tether," is a novelist, short story writer, and teaching artist. She graduated with an MFA at Wilkes University with a Bachelor of Arts in English and History from Misericordia University, and Master of Arts degrees in Museum Studies from Johns Hopkins University. Published works include, "A Dream," "Faith and Dandelion Seeds," and "Evermore." She writes thrillers, drama, speculative fiction, and mysteries that center on family, women, and BIPOC communities.

Blessing Odunyemi is a British-born Nigerian poet, writer, and musician. She was shortlisted for the 2023 Heritage of London Trust Poet for Places and longlisted for *Kinsman Quarterly's* African Diaspora Award. Her poem "Black Snow" is inspired by her childhood in Nigeria and the colonial ties to her UK home.

Jody T. Pratt, author of "Blueberry Pie," is from Sacramento, California. He has spent a lifetime consuming dark fiction in television and books, developing a taste for its misfortune and horror. He aims to elevate the genre of black thriller, suspense, and horror to become a force in the dark fiction genre. Pratt, who also powerlifts and competes in the super-heavyweight class, aspires to write in both television and film.

Quiana is the author of "Tough Meat," a work inspired by her life as a youth raised in Los Angeles. She is a "freestyle writing mama" of four who serves underprivileged youth. She has a Bachelor's degree in Developmental Psychology, and in her pastime, Quiana enjoys painting, watching comedies, and spending time with family.

Jana Ross, grand-prize winner of the African Diaspora Award, wrote "Clay People" and the poetry collection "Me and My Hair." She is a gifted poet and literary scholar inspired by artists like Gwendolyn Brooks, Virginia Woolf, FKA Twigs, and La Dispute. Ross aspires to connect with other writers, explore various poetry forms, and eventually publish her own book.

Abdulrazaq Salihu, from Niger State, Nigeria, is a member of the Hilltop Creative Arts Foundation and has won poetry contests like the Hilltop Creative Writing Award and Nigerian Prize for Teen Authors. Besides *Kinsman Quarterly*, Salihu's poetry has been recognized in magazines like the *Jupiter Review*, *Angime*, and *Grub Street Mag*. His powerful collection, "Exit Wounds," demonstrates sophisticated use of imagery, daring exploration of rhythm, and captivating emotional content.

Jon Jon Stefan, author of the poetry collection "Repatriate," serves as a community activist, confronting issues of poverty and systematic injustice in his town of Rochester. Stefan's upbringing in foreign missions instilled in him a passion for the disadvantaged and an appreciation for diverse cultures. His poetry focuses on the complexities of the human psyche and relationships that impact it.

Jonathan Chibuike Ukah wrote the powerful poetry collection "Blame the Gods." He is a graduate of English and Law living in the UK with his family. His poems have been featured (and will soon be featured) in *Strange Horizons*, *Atticus Review*, *Shift Literary Magazine of the University of Ringling*, *The Pierian*, and the *Journal of Undiscovered Poets*. He is a winner of the Voices of Lincoln Poetry Contest 2022 and has been recently nominated for the Pushcart Prize.

ACKNOWLEDGEMENTS

Special thanks to the founding Kinsman Quarterly team, whose contributions and support initiated a phenomenal launch to our mission to amplify diverse voices. Particularly, our board of directors; Yolanda Simpson, Angelica Anderson, and Thomas Franz. Thanks to our marketing and design team, who did extraordinary work on media designs; Anastasia Simone, Summer Greigh, Jay Lee, and Bobbie Jean Stanley.

There are not enough words to describe our gratitude to Dawn Leas, Co-Editor and founder of the Hammock Writer. She is an esteemed colleague and beloved friend. Likewise, we are grateful to those who supported the editing team; Sophia Obianamma Gabriel and Mildred J Mills.

We further extend our appreciation to the contributing poets; Wayne Benson Jr., Hess Love, Maitreyi Karanth, and Jon Jon Stefan. As well, for Akin Jeje, our literature director, who judged the first African Diaspora Award and selected such phenomenal winners among so many finalists.

Thanks to our advocacy director, Nicole Doyley, who was an incredible instrument of local support. We are also grateful for the consultants who helped us make important connections; David Hicks, the creative writing director of Wilkes University, Mentor Gregory Fletcher, and Maxwell Bauman. And much love to ongoing supporters like Jayne Jeje, Julie Danao-Salkin, and our newly appointed outreach director, Nicole Negrón. Much love to all!

www.ingramcontent.com/pod-product-compliance
Lightning Source LLC
Chambersburg PA
CBHW060558310726
48982CB00008B/1163/J

* 9 7 8 1 9 6 2 1 2 1 0 1 9 *